PE

THE

Tam Hoskyns has worked in TV and theatre for
years. She and her family live in London. *The Talking Cure* is her
first novel.

TAM HOSKYNS

———

THE TALKING CURE

PENGUIN BOOKS

PENGUIN BOOKS

Published by the Penguin Group
Penguin Books Ltd, 27 Wrights Lane, London W8 5TZ, England
Penguin Putnam Inc., 375 Hudson Street, New York, New York 10014, USA
Penguin Books Australia Ltd, Ringwood, Victoria, Australia
Penguin Books Canada Ltd, 10 Alcorn Avenue, Toronto, Ontario, Canada M4V 3B2
Penguin Books (NZ) Ltd, 182–190 Wairau Road, Auckland 10, New Zealand

Penguin Books Ltd, Registered Offices: Harmondsworth, Middlesex, England

First published by Hamish Hamilton 1997
Published in Penguin Books 1998
1 3 5 7 9 10 8 6 4 2

Copyright © Tam Hoskyns, 1997
All rights reserved

The moral right of the author has been asserted

Printed in England by Clays Ltd, St Ives plc

Prologue

It happened when I was sitting in Bill's car. Waiting for him, as usual. He was after a story somewhere in Bloomsbury and we couldn't find a parking space. So I was keeping watch. On a double yellow line.

I had a sixth sense about that journey before we even set off. The kind of sense that I only used to feel with my twin, that something was going to happen and I had to be there. I was meant to see it, I know. I have no doubt about that.

And if I hadn't been looking for it, I dare say I'd have noticed the incident anyway, or at least noticed the eventual body, but I noticed the killer too, because I was very focused on the old boy as he was trying to cross the road.

He looked so broken up. Like a child's discarded toy. He had sacking tied around his feet for shoes, he shivered uncontrollably inside his rough tweed overcoat, his face was hidden under a haystack of matted grey hair and he was filthy. He was waving two white sticks in the air, white for a blind man, so that traffic stopped for him.

He stumbled across the road towards me, brandishing the sticks fantastically, enjoying his meagre power. But then he fell against the bonnet of my car and his face swung round to curse me, or to curse the air, or whoever was there. As he lifted his face towards me, I saw that in fact he was a woman.

The face was extraordinary. Fine-featured. High-cheekboned. Big-eyed. Even in rage and age, filthy as it was, with its milky, opaque eyes, it was quite beautiful.

I was about to get out of my car and guide her on to the pavement, perhaps even slip her some money, when another woman approached her. I couldn't see this other woman's face. She had approached from behind me and she was too close up in my rear-view mirror for me to see much more than her coat. An elegant coat, well-cut. She breezed past my window like a bird, moving swiftly. I had the impression that she was rushing to help the old woman on to the steep kerb, but although she had taken the old woman's arm, and appeared to be engaged in some kind of effort with her (she had her back to me and was masking the old woman almost completely with her coat), it was very soon apparent that she had not helped at all. She had in fact hindered. She had left the old woman to fall to the ground, racing on as fast as she could without breaking into a run.

I got out of the car then, when the smart young woman had disappeared from view, to find the old woman bleeding profusely, her worn tweed coat absorbing the dark liquid like a sponge. She was already dead, her eyes staring their opaque blue at me, her body limp as cloth. No pulse.

I held her in my arms, as I had held my own stillborn boy, ten years previously. Bloody and dead. She must have died from the shock before the knife had even cut through the thick of the tweed.

Now the absurd thing was that because I had touched her, and because I had seen a woman, not a man, do this deed, I had the irrational conviction that I would be accused. So I didn't report it. And since the old lady was already dead, I saw no sensible reason to risk reporting it. Instead, checking myself for any stain of her, I got back in the car, pulled away from the kerb and searched for a meter a few roads down.

I never reported it. This was, perhaps, the most regrettable thing I have ever failed to do, given the events that followed. I didn't even tell Bill. He would have wanted the story too much and I was too afraid. I searched the newspapers frantically for days afterwards, but there was no mention of it. If it hadn't been for my cowardice, she could have been caught then. Before she did any more harm. I could have caught her myself.

But at the time, my cowardice seemed as nothing compared with my perverse delight. There was an unwelcome part of me that found it all quite thrilling.

It wasn't long after this incident, this murder, that Howard telephoned. Only a week or so later. My mind was turning over dust like a detective's mind, wondering why a smart young woman would murder a poor old tramp who looked like a man but was in fact a woman. So when Howard turned up with his face beaten in, he somehow fitted into the same perplexed part of my brain where violence was done. And where the thrill was felt. Even then I knew that the two things were linked. Although I couldn't see how for months afterwards.

I

He was my third client. The first one gave up after four weeks, the second left the country after two. My supervisor said, did I think this was because of the thing I do of not saying what I think?

'Maybe it is,' I said.

'It creates a distance. You must stay close. Try to stay close,' he said.

As a child I used to think that staying close meant being nice. Now I know that it means admitting what you're most afraid to say, and hearing what they're most afraid to say, and staying side by side. Equals. You don't steal their power from them. And you don't give your own power away.

Why did I find this so hard?

My sister was unsurprised to hear of my failures when she dropped by. She was the expert, after all. She even laughed at me.

'Another triumph, eh, Mo?'

'Well . . .' I mumbled.

'What is it with you?' she said. 'You fail at everything.'

'We can't all win,' I said.

'Spoken like a loser if I ever heard one.'

You'd think that if you were doing as well as Kate, you'd be more generous.

'It's a different kind of therapy to yours, Kate. Less directive.'

'How fascinating,' she said, but didn't mean.

'Yes,' I said and meant.

Pause.

'I'll get the hang of it. If anyone else gives me a chance.'

But plainly she didn't think I would.

'Why don't you try Cognitive Behavioural?' she asked.

'Because I've only just started Person-Centred, Kate.'

'Person-Centred is for people-pleasers, Mo! Everyone knows that. Cowards who can't tell the truth. You're so scared of being disliked, aren't you?'

'Well . . .' I mumbled again.

'I wonder if it's really your thing at all,' she said. 'Therapy. Don't you?'

'Do you?'

'Mmm,' she said. 'And I have to tell you, so does Bill.'

In fact Howard called when I had given up hope of working in the field at all.

'I need some help,' he said.

'Who is this?'

It turned out I'd met him somewhere. I didn't remember. He reminded me.

'Oh, Kate's . . .' But I was thinking of Bill. Of what she'd said about him.

He was quiet. I knew that he knew that I still didn't know who he was.

'It was a big party,' I offered, excusing myself.

'You admired my tie, if that helps.'

It did help. He was a striking man, I recalled. Awesome, even. Tall. Dark. Grave. One of Picasso's naked, heavy-limbed women had wrapped herself round his tie, unbelonging as colour to stone. He might have been stone himself:

sculpted, carved, cold, contained so within the outline of himself.

'I remember,' I said. Bill had been away then, too. Bill was always away.

I had talked about my training then, apparently. At Kate's. Or so he said. Which was why he was calling me now. Was I practising yet? Could he make an appointment? Maybe tomorrow?

'Sure.'

Tomorrow was a stormy Monday in October, the London air thick with rain, clouds weighing so heavily up above that daylight had almost turned dark.

I rehearsed my opening lines so that they sounded spontaneous but they didn't, ever, and when I opened the door to him I was dumb.

He seemed no less awesome, more so, if anything, a giant of a man towering above me, his black umbrella killing the remaining light. At last he let it fold down, as though disarming himself, and allowed me to take him in.

His face was a mess. Cut. Swollen. Bruised. I think he attempted a smile but his top lip refused to comply.

'Hello,' he said with forced cheerfulness, eyes avoiding me.

I don't remember what I said, or how he came to be sitting in the room I had prepared for my practice, months previously. I only remember thinking how serious this was, how, despite all the training in the world, I would perhaps always feel inadequate to the task of another person's life in my hands. Kate would laugh at that. But then, we're different.

I remember noticing that he sat with his back to the window, blocking out what little light there was.

*

Bill was away. I didn't know where. I missed him. We lived in a large house then, one that anticipated children who still refused our efforts to conceive them. Occasionally their unborn spirits would enter, softly and strangely padding out the place with their bulk, but only when sleep had persistently eluded me. More often, I could hear nothing but our own echoing lives bouncing back at us like hollow balls from the walls. When alone, I couldn't even hear this. I was frightened there, alone.

I was very nervous that particular day, even before Howard arrived; I know I must have been because I remember I checked my exits, and tested the panic button wired to the burglar alarm. And I think I even prayed. Uncharacteristically. I don't know what I feared, but my tutor's words rang loud in my ears. 'Never see anyone in your private practice alone unless you feel really secure.' She was adamant.

A hot feeling of shame coursed through me. Words like 'impulsive' and 'irresponsible' welcomed me home. I knew that I was taking an almighty risk, that anything could happen, but I also knew that this was my last chance. The big adventure of my dull, barren life. Nothing would stop me.

Funny. My heart is racing even now, as I look back. Standing on the edge of that decision, which had already been made, and yet which had to be made over and over again. Even when it was all over and his great cold back was turned away from me, I had to decide again that I had done the right thing.

Because I knew more certainly than I had ever known anything that as soon as I stepped into the unfamiliar terrain of this particular man, nothing would ever be the same.

Although I had done my training and had read a forestful, as he sat there waiting I could only remember a suggestion to forget the lot. Put theory aside and engage wholly with your client's particular life, I had heard or read or even written somewhere.

'So . . .' I ventured, leaving him to finish off.

Silence.

I felt instantly crowded with fears. I tried to put them aside, to be available to this third client of mine, but they waited for me and called out still.

Breathe, I told myself, and made a mental note to return to therapy myself.

'So . . . what? Mo.'

The way he said my name, thumped it on the end like that, implied a menace somehow, a desire to intimidate me.

Leave it for now, I told myself.

'So! I'm all yours. I'll need to ask you a few rudimentary questions at some stage during our first session but essentially the time is yours. All sixty minutes of it!'

Why so jocular? Relax.

A longer silence this time. He was looking me up and down.

How like a game of chess, I heard myself think. Move by move.

I wondered if he was playing a sort of power-game. But I hardly knew the man. Looking me up and down might have been a mark of respect. I was frightened, that was all, and I was looking for reasons why.

Calm down, Mo, I ordered, but then I caught myself. And don't repress. Admit and put to one side. I am fucking terrified.

'I'm rather wary,' he said, picking a small particle of dust from his knee.

I emitted what I thought was an encouraging grunt to assure him that I'd heard his first tentative disclosure, but it effectively silenced him.

9

'It's new to me, all this . . .'

I didn't believe him. God knows why. A hunch.

'I'm wary too,' I confessed, keen to draw him out.

He didn't want to be drawn.

'Well, more nervous than wary, but –'

'Oh?' he suddenly asked, looking up quizzically. 'Why are you nervous? Are you nervous of me?'

I shrugged vaguely, very unwilling to say.

He looked back at his knee, as if admiring the weave of his expensive suit, restored to its former glory now without that speck of dust.

'You know, Howard, I really want to ask you what you've done to your face.'

'I thought this was my hour?'

'Sorry?'

'It's my hour, isn't it?'

'Yes.'

'I'll decide what I tell you and when.'

'And I don't think there was anything in what I said that implied a demand to the contrary.'

I wanted to add that short of inflicting grievous bodily harm, it was unlikely that I could exert any control over his disclosures whatsoever, but I checked myself in time.

'You have no right to interrogate me,' he said. 'Do you understand? You're here to serve, not to rule.'

I remember feeling unsurprised at that moment that someone had beaten him up, but I can just about forgive myself now. I knew so little of this whole process then, and even less about Howard North himself. And besides, assumptions are natural enough. The skill is in admitting them.

In the silence which followed, I dared to ask:

'I'm wondering what happened there.'

I was doing everything by the book. Even down to 'I'm wondering'.

'What "happened" there?' he said drily, mocking my tone.

'In that little exchange we just had?' I ploughed on through his ridicule: 'Because, you see, I felt some misunderstanding there. I expressed my desire to ask you a question – some curiosity about the state of your face – a natural concern, I would say –'

'I'm sure you would.'

'But it seems to me that you perceived my concern as – in some way – presumptuous? An imposition?'

I was careful to intone this as a question.

'I perceive most of your psycho-speak as an imposition, Mo.'

'Uh-huh . . .'

Nothing if not direct.

'I don't want to listen to your textbook jargon labouring under the guise of "concern", when it's plain as day you're not really interested in *me*. Do you understand?'

'Uh-huh.'

Only too well. Back came the fear again.

'Don't give me this odious fake-sincerity lark you all do. It disgusts me.'

He paused for my response. I realized that I had only heard his tone of voice, and not the words themselves. Not the meaning. Fear was in my way.

'I'm sorry – could you repeat that, please?'

He narrowed his eyes suspiciously, as if doubting that I could be quite as inattentive as I seemed.

'I'm here to be heard,' he said, more plainly.

'Yes,' I agreed, following that much, at least.

'It would assist me greatly if you paid attention to what I say, therefore.'

'Right.'

'Furthermore, I am here to be heard clearly – that is, either with genuine concern, or with a rational mind, or both.'

'Uh-huh . . .'

'I am not here to be patronized by the kind of half-baked pseudo-integrity that so plagues your profession these days.'

He left a silence, during which he sat so rigidly still that he might have been a model of himself.

'Do you know quite a lot about my profession?' I asked.

'Enough,' he said.

'Why choose a novice like me? Or was it a deliberate choice?'

He chose not to answer me. Which was an answer in itself. Here was a man who made every choice deliberately, who weighed up every tiny speck of dust.

'Do you work in this profession yourself?' was my next question.

It had already left my lips before I remembered that it wasn't my business to interrogate him. That I was there to serve, not to rule.

'If you ask me one more of your idiotically direct questions . . .' he yelled.

'I'm sorry. OK? I'm sorry. No more questions, I swear.'

I suddenly needed Bill. I wanted him home. I wanted my husband home.

Howard released a controlled sigh, drawing my attention back to him.

'I'll do the talking now,' he said. 'First, I have to fill you in. I can't tell you anything about this –' he pointed to his face – 'this ridiculous little uninteresting scratch, until you know all about this –' He thumped his heart with a tight fist, holding the moment theatrically, daring me to speak, which needless to say I did.

'Can I just stop you there?'

He sighed with exasperation.

'What now?'

'I just want to be sure I've understood you so far –' I pleaded, and I launched into my textbook paraphrase, knowing that I tempted his wrath.

'You feel that my concern for you isn't real, that it's not genuine somehow. You object fiercely to my questioning you. You find my behaviour towards you invasive, or imposing, as though everything I say is out of a textbook rather than because I care about you, is that right?'

'"The paraphrase",' he sneered.

'Is it accurate?'

'You tell me,' he challenged.

'I think there's some truth in it, yes, I'm sorry to admit. I don't know you yet, so I'm using what modest skills I have to speed up the process.'

Pause.

'May I go on?'

'You mean there's more?'

'I understand that you want to tell me about your deeper feelings – your heart –' I mirrored his gesture, thumping my own heart with a fist.

He interrupted, his own fist involuntarily back at his chest.

'I want to tell you about me!' It was almost a shout. He stopped still, as if somewhat surprised by himself, then explained more soberly, 'I have to tell you the story so far, the sequence of events, before I can tell you how I scratched my face.'

'OK,' I said inadequately, moved by the sudden passion in him.

He waited a while, clearly expecting some further response

from me, something to kick up against, but I was not forthcoming.

When he was sure, at last, of my more sentient attention, he began.

'There was only me. And her.'

He was studying me already for some trace of emotion, before I knew even who or what he meant.

'My little sister was drowned when she was tiny,' he said, his own emotion absent as air. 'I mean, tiny.'

He held his hands apart to indicate her approximate size. About a foot and a half. Then one hand tilted slightly, as though to cup her head. As though to say what could never be said.

'So very small, she was . . .'

Even my breath seemed indelicate against her tiny frame, but holding it in felt like a kind of drowning too.

He bent his head down to listen to her heart or her breath or both, I didn't know which, I didn't ask, but he smiled unfathomably.

I thought of the old woman and her absent pulse. He looked straight up at me, as if sensing her.

'What?' he demanded, dropping the baby like a ball.

'Nothing.'

'What happened?'

'Nothing.' But he didn't believe me. 'I remembered something. That's all.'

'What?'

'I don't want to talk about it.'

He punished me with a silence, which I broke.

'She really mattered to you, didn't she?' I asked.

He sneered at me contemptuously.

'God almighty,' he said. 'You're the limit.'

'I'm sorry?'

'I don't think this is going to work,' he said wearily.

'Why not?' I asked, the panic rising in my voice.

'I really can't tolerate this pseudo-insightfulness of yours – this pseudo-everything of yours! You're like a walking textbook! Is this what they taught you at school? I thought you admired Neville Hoare?'

'I do! I –'

'Surely not! Would Hoare approve of this? Be yourself, can't you?'

'I wasn't aware that I was being anyone else.'

'There's a great deal you're not aware of, Higgs.'

'Such as?' I demanded hotly.

'Don't you see?' he asked. 'If I'm going to reveal myself, the intimate details of my life, to another person, then it has to be on my terms.'

'But it's on my territory.'

'So?'

'So it would be courteous if you checked your terms with me before we agree to proceed.'

He looked surprised. For a moment, I think, I had his respect.

'Very well. My terms are that you remain silent unless you can be yourself. I don't want a "therapist", I want a human being.'

'And the reality is that you've got a human, being a therapist.'

He looked at me with unutterable contempt then. I had surpassed the credible. He could only close his eyes in response, as if to eliminate me entirely from his world.

'Joke,' I apologized.

He reopened his eyes, somewhat reluctantly, squinting in the suddenness of sun. Then he got to his feet.

'Do you mind if I let down this blind?'

'Go ahead,' I said, flattered to be considered at all.

When he was sitting in the armchair again and I had switched on the desk-lamp so that I could see his face, he said:

'You're an intelligent woman, Mo. That's the part I want.'

Something about the way he said this froze my blood. Or was it the way he looked at me – as though he could see exactly what he wanted from me. Something that I couldn't see.

It was with sudden intimacy that he leaned forward to confide the next:

'I was there when she found her.'

I waited for more but none came.

'Who?' I asked, humanly curious and not denying it.

'I don't know how I was there,' he said, ignoring me. 'That's what perplexes me. If I hadn't done it, why was I there? How did I know where to look?' He paused briefly, scouring his memory. 'Or was I not looking for her at all? Perhaps I was just – there? Was I just – in the area?'

'Which area, Howard? Where?'

He glanced at me irritably, as if to explain himself would be a tiresome inconvenience that I might spare him if I had even a modicum of skill.

'The area of the pond,' he said acerbically.

'Uh-huh . . .'

'The pond where she was drowned.'

'Was drowned or drowned?'

'Eh?'

'She was drowned there or she drowned there? There's a big difference.'

He looked at me as if I'd said something remarkably profound.

'Good God. How extraordinary.'

He seemed suddenly wrapped up, like glass, in impenetrable layers of thought.

'Is it?' I probed.

He looked up at me.

'Is it extraordinary?' I asked.

'I've never seen that before,' he said, looking through me. 'How have I never seen that?'

'What?'

'She never even allowed that possibility. It might have been an accident! Why not? Isn't that an obvious possibility? And yet we never even considered it. Why on earth not?'

He was asking me directly, staring me straight in the face, but somehow looking through me, too, at the tiny drowned child in the pond.

Then he turned away and laughed to himself. A sad, broken laugh.

'She knew it was murder. That's why.' He paused to realize more. 'And how? Because she did it herself. I didn't do it. She did. How could she know, otherwise, if she hadn't done it herself? Or did she watch me do it? Is that how she knew it was me? And if so, if she watched me do it, then she was complicit too; she did it with me, she was guilty too.'

He fell silent, as if into water himself. I broke the surface of it.

'I think I follow,' I said. 'Your little sister was drowned, but you don't know who by. Possibly by you. Or her? Is – "she" – your mother, then, or –'

'Yes, of course,' he said briskly, covering my voice with his own, in case anyone should hear, then whispering, 'My mother. Of course. Yes . . .'

He sank into silence again. I felt like a deep-sea fisherman hauling in the dead weight of a whale. I wanted more, much more, than I had grasped so far.

'So . . . your sister was drowned by someone? Your mother or . . . ? Or possibly you? Or . . . ?'

He wasn't helping. He wasn't there. He was where it was happening. Then. Not here or now at all.

'I just don't know,' he said, shaking his head.

I shook mine too, sympathetically.

'The difficulty is that we scarcely spoke of it again. My memories on the subject are so distant. Vague. I was only five, for God's sake. And yet I remember it bound us so tight, so close together, the collusion of it, the confusion of it, the mutual forgiveness, somehow, the mutual uncertainty of it . . . How will I ever know for sure?'

'I don't know,' I said, keen to remind him I was there.

He looked up at me then and seemed startled, caught off-guard, as if suddenly re-entering the three-dimensional world.

'So that's my first memory,' he announced somewhat formally. 'Or non-memory. My first encounter with the Plague. I call it the Plague.'

'The Plague being . . . ?'

'What?' he snapped.

I was very careful to sound like a human being:

'What's the Plague?'

'If you say a word of this to anyone . . .' he warned.

'It's confidential.' I nodded blithely. 'Except –'

'Except no one,' he said.

'Well, I will actually have a supervisor, in fact, who –'

'No one, Mo.'

He was at once intensely present, the black circle around his luminous grey-blue eyes underlining, like ink, his emphatic words.

'No one.'

I had the feeling that he was holding on to me, if not

physically then mentally. I might as well have been dangling from his grasp. I couldn't move. Only when he was satisfied that I had heard his instructions with every single cell of my being did he let me go.

The reminder of the session was a strain, perhaps because he'd said too much too soon for either of us. Certainly I was full up. The only further disclosure he made, that undressing his sister had been a curious pleasure for him, was one too many for me. Murder sufficed for one day.

He seemed concerned to emphasize that there had been no perversion in this curious pleasure of his. No abuse. He had simply been 'interested' because she didn't have what he had 'down there' – just that funny little line, as he used to call it. As a boy he had even looked it up in a library book to put his mind at rest.

'Howard,' I said, 'I'm aware that we're running out of time, so can I just stop you there and tie up a few loose ends before we close, and then next week we'll have more time and we'll be able to –'

'Next week?'

'Yes.'

'Can't I see you tomorrow?'

'Er – well –'

'The day after?'

Pause.

'Can I call you about that?'

Another pause.

'Very well.'

'Which brings me to the practicalities – I'm going to need a contact number from you, for a start.'

He handed me his card.

'Thank you.'

I went through my rehearsed routine – what kind of therapist I was, when I liked to be paid, whether he had any medical history that I ought to know about, etc.

He paid me my modest fee. I showed him to the front door. It was raining again outside, the sky as unpredictable as North himself. He hovered in the doorway, huge again as he fumbled with his umbrella. It flew up like a bird, carrying him out on to the top step.

'Goodbye, Mo.'

2

As soon as Howard had gone I started shaking, almost feverishly, as if I'd been infected by him. His word 'plague' came
to mind. I knew that the stabbing in Bloomsbury had set my
nerves on edge, and would do for some time. And I knew that
another client was an important, loaded thing for me, that I
had a lot at stake, a lot to prove. Especially to Kate. And Bill.
But this? I was a caricature of fear, my bowels lurching into
interminable action. Every tiny sound sped the adrenalin
through my body like a drug, perversely pleasurable.

That same evening I received three anonymous telephone
calls. None of them so much as whispered to me. Or breathed,
even. Was this North? Or was it the murderess, intimidating
witnesses? Or was it just Bill at last, sorry at last, loving and
missing me and trying hard to get through on his useless mobile
telephone?

Sadly, although this last would seem the most likely scenario
to any outsider, to me it felt the least likely of all. He called
less and less often as the years went by. I was not so much a
lover as a burden to him now. He would admit that, too. He
would admit to his disappointment in me and I would listen
almost politely and then I would feel a sharp needling pain as
if he had stuck a hat-pin in me, so thin that at first I didn't
feel it sink in. Then there'd be a row, of course. And then I'd
go back to thinking how much happier he would be with Kate.
If Kate wasn't married to Cliff.

At midnight the doorbell rang. I assumed that it was Bill, returning as suddenly as he had left. I only checked my impulse to answer at the last moment, as I stood in the hall.

Why would Bill ring the bell? Hands full? Lost his keys?

The visiting shape was vague through the opaque glass of the door, while I was quite clear in the bright light of the hall. I moved slowly towards the door, half-amused by my antics and half-petrified. I pressed my face against the peep-hole, peering through the tiny convex lens.

Nothing. Pitch blackness. Whoever it was had covered the lens with their hand.

Then the telephone rang. For the fourth time.

My heart beat so loud now it was like a great drum in my ears. I backed away from the door. Slowly. I realized that I hadn't double-locked it, that, unconsciously hoping for Bill's imminent return, I had in fact left it unbolted so that he could get in without waking me up. Perhaps whoever it was had seen me doing this and was in full possession of the fact that only a Yale lock, a fragile, kickable-in Yale lock, stood between me and him.

When I was almost out of view I ran up the stairs, pausing on the landing to listen. I don't know what I expected to hear above the telephone, which continued to ring. I crept into the bedroom, as if my stealth would somehow conceal my obvious whereabouts.

I didn't dare answer the telephone. I could no longer fool myself that the persistent caller was Bill. To answer it now seemed plainly dangerous.

I picked up the receiver and put it down immediately.

Then I called the police. It took an age to get through, and the doorbell rang again. I sat on the bed, trembling with the thrill and the fear of it, waiting to be saved.

A few minutes later I heard the lock turn. Someone had opened the door. I listened above the din of my heart for a clue. Where was he? Standing in the hall? Waiting for my first move? Silence. I held my breath but my heart was unstoppable. *Where was he?*

Then he spoke.

'Are you up?'

It was Bill.

I breathed. Then I went downstairs, smiling mildly, as though everything was all right.

'Hi,' I said easily, kissing his cheek.

'Sorry I'm so late.'

'I wasn't expecting you, early or late. It doesn't make much odds.'

'Right.'

'In fact these days I hardly dare expect you back at all.'

He glared at me, and then passed through into the living-room. I followed.

'Sorry,' I said.

He said, 'Give me a break.'

'You've just had a break,' I said. And then I said, 'I need you, Bill.'

He let out a great big sigh which told me all I needed to know.

'I've got a new client,' I said, changing my tone. 'A very clever man.'

'Oh, yes,' he acknowledged, but he was only half-listening.

'The trouble is, Bill, you say you want love, you want commitment, but when I give it to you, you just throw it back in my face.'

'What are you talking about?'

'I'm talking about you.'

He had just stood up to pour himself a drink when the police arrived. I'd forgotten about them. I felt rather ashamed and rather relieved and greeted them cheerfully. They had saved me, after all, from facing up to the truth.

'I'm so sorry, it was my husband – I thought he was an intruder but –'

'Very good, miss. Could we come in for a moment?'

And the two of them eased their way into the hall, eyeing Bill suspiciously.

'What the bloody hell's going on?' said Bill.

'Can we just take a statement from you, sir?' one said, his pen already poised. 'Only we have to take a statement now.' And the other constable took me into the next room.

After our respective tales had been told, they advised caution in opening the door without a door-chain, congratulated me for using the peep-hole, and were gone.

'Using the peep-hole?' asked Bill, pouring himself a Scotch.

'When you rang the bell.'

'I didn't ring the bell.'

I slept atrociously, slapping Bill with fitful arms. I was weighing things up. I had to make a decision the next morning about Howard North. When to see him again. It should have been 'whether' not 'when'.

At six o'clock I slipped out of bed, kissing Bill's face when he least minded it, cushioned on the pillow, asleep. Dead to the world.

I thought of her little body. Floppy, wet and dead.

I sat at my desk with a cup of coffee, black and thick as bitumen, and flicked through the tentative notes I had made.

I'll get better at this, I told myself, as I searched for some clue.

I felt more like a detective than a therapist as I tried to piece together the man's beaten face, his dead sister, his mother, and what it was he wanted from me.

Bill shuffled in at eight o'clock, squinting in the shock of sunlight through the window, his yellow hair everywhere.

'What are you doing?'

'Just working.'

I resented the objection he was about to make.

'At what?'

'Darling, I did actually tell you last night that I have a new client now –'

'Yes, I know. But he's not here, is he? What can you do? It's eight o'clock in the morning.' He was building up to nagging me.

'I can read my notes, I can ... think ... I can try to –'

'He sounds like a sicko, Mo, a bloody psychopath.'

'Just because he might possibly have rung the bell? Is that so sick?'

'You can't "save" him, you know.'

'Who says I'm going to save him?'

'Isn't that what all therapists do . . . ?'

'And anyway, who says it was him last night? It could've been anyone.'

'Sure,' he said drily. 'Why pick on the psychopaths?'

I didn't respond.

'I know – why don't you send him to see Kate? Get him live on her TV show. She'll sort him out. She's the expert, isn't she?'

He knew this would hurt.

'Hardly,' I muttered sourly, unable to credit her with any talent at all.

'Or, better still, have him certified.'

I put down my pen, swung round in my chair and glared at him furiously.

'What d'you want?'

'Nothing.'

'Come on. Tell me. What?'

'Forget it. You're in a mood.'

'I'm not in a mood. What do you want?' I insisted, spoiling for a fight.

'Doesn't matter . . .' he muttered wearily, shuffling out again.

'Jesus!' I shouted. But he didn't respond, sensibly enough.

I was livid. I wanted a bloody great row, I realized. I wanted to hear myself justify to Bill all my reasons for a second session with North, against all his best arguments.

I tried to understand why Howard North was so important to me. I couldn't. I didn't have the insight, or the hindsight, then.

THINGS TO DO, I wrote on my A4 pad.

Top of the list went CALL STEPH HARRIGAN.

Do things by the book, I told myself: therapist, supervisor.

Next on the list went CALL SUPERVISOR, and, although I intended to, I knew it would take me a while. I was too excited to risk losing North. And I was also too scared. I'd been warned, threatened even, to speak to nobody.

I stared out at the garden in defeat. The autumn leaves were dripping from the stag's-horn sumach like fresh red blood. A big fat jay was sitting on a branch of it. He seemed almost to be the violator, spilling the blood himself.

Ugly birds, I thought. Lonely scavengers. I was feeling more antipathy towards this bird than I had ever felt towards a bird

26

in my life. It reminded me of someone, I realized. I was in there somewhere, but it wasn't just me. The flash of brilliant cold blue reminded me of North.

What does Kate know about him? I wondered. Maybe I'll ask her.

After breakfast with Bill, who was punishingly uncommunicative behind his newspaper, reading his own article about 'The First Grey Hair' and cursing his copyist, I called Howard North.

'What time?' Bill was intensely irritated.

'Why does it matter what time? I wasn't expecting you back today, anyway.'

'Listen, this is my home and if I –'

'Oh, don't start this again.'

'No, listen –'

'No, I bloody won't.'

I went into the kitchen. He pursued me hotly.

'Don't just walk away!'

It was a small kitchen, but he managed to pace up and down in it.

I said very quietly, so as not to agitate him further, 'There's nothing to worry about.'

He stopped, his eyes searching mine. I looked away, because in truth there was plenty to worry about that he might see.

'I get in at midnight, you're being very weird but you won't tell me why, you've called the police after someone's rung the bell and put their hand over the peep-hole and someone else has phoned up four times without speaking to you, I ask you about this guy Leslie North –'

'Howard.'

'Leslie Howard –'

'Howard Nor –'

'Whatever the fuck he's called!' he bellowed. 'I ask you about him and you won't tell me a single bloody thing!'

'I've told you his name. I shouldn't even have told you his name.'

'You're off with me, you can't sleep, you hit me all night, you tell me you're scared but you won't say why since you saw this guy, or you say you don't know why, and now you invite him back! Without even seeing whoever you need to see or talking to me about it or anything!'

'I can't talk to you about it, can I? It's confidential.'

'Crap.'

'It's not crap. It's part of the job, Bill. A very important part.'

'But I'm not going to tell anyone, am I? Who am I going to tell?'

He almost pleaded with me. I was reminded of playground secrets at school.

I said, 'That's not the point,' because it wasn't.

'Well, I'm sorry, but I think the whole thing stinks.'

He kicked the fridge door.

'Yes, well, you would, wouldn't you? Because you can't stand me being interested in anyone but you, can you? So you can reject me all the time –'

'Bollocks.'

'You're secretly quite glad we can't have children, aren't you, because it means you get all my attention, twenty-four hours a day.'

'Are you serious?'

'But now suddenly that's threatened, isn't it? Because I've got clients now. Thank God it's only clients, not kids, or what would you be like?'

'You should've stuck to architecture, love. You can't do people, can you?'

'Other way round, in fact.'

'You can't do either, in fact.'

3

Bill left me unforgiven in the kitchen, slamming the front door so hard that the whole house shook.

In the afternoon Kate dropped by, minutes before Howard was due. It was the second time that month. She didn't usually drop by. Usually she rang to make an appointment a few weeks in advance. Or, more usually still, I would ring her and she'd try to fit me in. Twice in one month was keen.

'Mo,' she said. I often thought she was saying 'No' when in fact she was saying 'Mo'. An inherent order seemed to lurk somewhere inside her emphasis.

'What a surprise,' I said, not altogether pleased. I leaned forward to kiss her but she pulled away, wincing slightly. It was then that I noticed.

'What have you done to your face?'

'Nothing.'

'It's swollen.'

'No,' she said lightly. 'I've just got make-up on.'

'Why?'

'Why what?'

'Why have you got make-up on?'

'Why shouldn't I?'

'Because you hate it.'

'So?' She stumbled, which was odd for Kate. 'I've come to like it.'

'I see,' I said. 'Very nice.'

'Oh, for goodness' sake, Mo – I haven't come round to discuss the merits of make-up with you!'

No, I thought. You've come round to see Bill.

'What do you want?'

'Look, I'm really sorry to – not to warn you … I just wondered if you could do me the most enormous favour.'

'What?'

'It's just – it's half-term and I've got to reshoot an interview and –'

'No,' I said, like she says Mo. I glanced at the carload of children she had sweetly brought round for me, poor barren aunt.

'Well, thanks,' she said bitterly, 'I knew I could count on you.'

'I'm busy,' I said. I was longing to tell her. My trump card. Mr North.

'You seem busy,' she said.

'My new client is due any minute now.' I tossed this lightly at her.

She stared at me in uneasy disbelief. How she betrayed herself.

'Your new client?' she said uncomfortably. 'What new client? You never told me you had a new client, Mo.'

'Why should I?' I asked blithely, reinforced by this tiny success.

'No reason.' She paused. 'Except you're my twin. We didn't used to have secrets, did we?'

'We've always had secrets, Kate.'

'Well, professional secrets, of course. To disclose them would be unethical.'

'Exactly,' I concurred, placing my ethical secrets in the same professional league as her own.

She looked at me with a familiar mixture of hatred and pain.

'I have another client, Kate. Aren't you pleased for me?'

'What's his name?' she asked, unable to be pleased.

'Who says it's a he?'

'Well, is it?'

I longed to resist her, just once.

'Yes, Kate. It's a he.'

At that very moment Howard approached in his car, slowing down as if to park but then suddenly changing his mind and driving on, driving straight past us down the road.

Kate turned to see what I was looking at, her eyes following his car.

'Is that him?'

I didn't answer. Her face was full of unexpected rage.

'*Is that him?*' she bellowed, but then she saw herself in my face, staring back bewildered at her.

'I'd better go,' she said.

And she did, without saying goodbye. Screaming off in her black BMW.

He chose the same seat in front of the window, his face in shadow again, the sun bright in the garden outside.

'Hello, Textbook.' He grinned playfully as I sat down opposite him.

I smiled. How harmless he seemed in the warm afternoon light. Surely he couldn't be last night's terrorist?

'You seem . . . happy? Today?'

'Ha-pp-y!' He said the word as if it was foreign, something new to learn, somewhat puzzling. 'To-day?'

'Mock on,' I invited, good-humouredly. His face clouded over.

'Was that Kate?' he demanded.

'On the doorstep?' I asked. He simply glared at me, waiting for my reply. 'Yes,' I said.

'Does she know I'm seeing you?'

'Of course not.'

'Are you sure?'

'Quite sure.'

'Good.'

He was silent.

'You seem very troubled, Howard, by the thought of Kate.'

But then he seemed instantly untroubled, as if to conceal the very thing I'd observed so plainly in him.

'No!' He smiled broadly. 'Not troubled at all!'

'I'm wondering if perhaps it's a little confusing for you that Kate and I look so much alike?'

'Perhaps.'

'Do you know her particularly well?'

'Is that your business?'

'No. Probably not. Although it concerns me, certainly.'

'She thinks she knows me particularly well,' he said drily.

'Uh-huh.'

'The arrogance of idiots. Always so blind and so sure.'

'Strong words.'

'True words. Can we move on from your twin sister, charming though she is?'

'It's your hour,' I conceded, putting curiosity aside.

We fell into a well of extraordinary silence that seemed to echo back through his life. I sensed an almost inexpressible grief swallow up the room as his eyes searched mine. How could I find words that would adequately answer a sorrow like this?

He breathed in deeply but quietly, releasing the air with even, measured control.

'I feel I understand your silence better than your words,' I confessed.

'What do you understand of my silence?' he challenged defiantly.

'Something of your – sadness?'

'What sadness?'

'I don't know. I only know something of the measure of it.'

'What does it "measure", then?'

'Oh, Howard, I don't know. In silence perhaps I can see you better because you aren't pouncing on every word I say!' I said this without edge, since it was true that his silence had won a small piece of my heart. But I said it with strength, for once unusually fearless of him.

He half-smiled at me.

'Very good,' he said.

'I wish I didn't feel you were marking me out of ten all the time,' I said, more spontaneously still. 'I find it such an obstacle to the progress of our relationship.'

'What progress?'

'Precisely!'

He smiled again.

'You're on form today,' he said, allowing a score of roughly eight, I guessed.

A long silence.

'I was thinking of a woman I loved,' he said, eventually.

I didn't say anything.

'And lost.'

I made the tiniest movement with my head which he might, if he wanted, mistake for a nod. I had finally seen that I must answer his quiet, hidden language with my own if he was to trust me at all.

'She killed herself in the end. This year. Ten years later to the day. She left me everything, for some reason. After all that time apart. I thought she had forgotten me, but amongst those pathetically humble possessions of hers were her diaries. And amongst the detailed documentation of her diaries were her frequent confessions of love. For me. She was full of love for me. Which was how I found out, how the question asked itself all over again.'

I waited.

'I was glad to learn she loved me, after so many years of doubt, but what I wasn't at all glad to learn was . . .'

He looked at me, then closed his eyes, breathed out, shook his head.

'I must be mad,' he said.

'Why?'

Pause.

'Let me start again.'

Pause.

'It's very – it's problematic to communicate one's . . . one's life.'

I waited patiently.

'I might do better to begin at the beginning and work my way through.' He thought about this for a while. 'You see, I have a very particular reason for seeking your help, which unfortunately I can't explain to you without frightening you off. I have to come at it in the right – from the right direction, you see.'

I didn't see, but nor did I say so. The less I said, the more he revealed himself.

'There's a mystery to solve, if you like. That's a good way of putting it. And I need your help in solving it. I can't ever seem to get to the bottom of it. I need an ally, that's what I really need.'

35

I nodded as indiscernibly as I dared without seeming contrived.

'The most important thing for you to understand is that . . . is . . .' He trailed off, losing his conviction again. 'I've done this so many times.'

'What, exactly?'

'This! All this talking it through! Trying to make sense of it. Trying to believe in this therapy thing. It never bloody works.' He paused, as if thinking better of his petulant defeat. 'But one has to believe in something, I suppose – and God seems very unwilling to make his presence felt in my life.'

I thought I knew why most gods would avoid Howard North. A god is a god, unlikely to kow-tow to exacting mortal terms like his.

'They thought my father killed Cassie, in the end.'

'Cassie?'

'Cassandra. My sister. Because he left the country so soon after the funeral. And never came back. Perhaps my mother put the idea into their heads, as a kind of revenge. Who knows? At first they believed it to be an accident, which for some reason my mother could never allow . . .'

'She never allowed that it might have been an accident.'

It was my first return to textbook technique, but he didn't seem to notice, or if he did, he didn't mind.

'Odd, that, isn't it? One might imagine that a mother's love would persuade her of an accident where there was none, or where there was in fact real malice, but not the other way round. If that makes any sense at all.'

'Uh-huh.'

'In the worst-case scenario, if we postulate that I did in fact kill my little sister, and that my mother did in fact see me do

36

it, how might one expect a mother to behave? Or if she didn't see me do it but assumed that I had done it, how might she then behave? Or if she had done it herself, and I had found her immediately after the deed, how differently might she behave then?'

We both wondered, although he had clearly wondered so often before that he seemed to be hoping more for my insight than for his own.

'The possibilities are endless,' I said.

'But what possibility crossed your mind so clearly just then?' His sharpness tripped me up.

'I was thinking about power,' I admitted.

'Say more.'

'I don't know your mother.'

'But you know your own.'

'Exactly. And every mother is different. We're all unique.'

'Talk about your own mother, then. There may be something in it, something I might see that I . . . do – please . . .'

'Power. That's all. Mothers enjoy power over their children when they lack it significantly elsewhere.'

'Which she did, most certainly.'

'So if she wanted your fear, your submission to her power, whether you did it or not, she'd behave judgementally, she'd make you work for her approval, for her faith in you. You'd want that more than anything else, wouldn't you, as a small boy? Her belief in you, in your basic goodness. Your lovable-ness. You'd need that.'

'Yes,' he said.

'Everyone needs that.'

'Yes,' he said again, in a small, quiet voice.

'You look sad,' I said.

The sadness filled up the room. I felt overwhelmed by it, but he seemed relatively unaware, determinedly unaffected, even oblivious to his own consuming grief.

'Of course it has crossed my mind that my father might have been the guilty one – that my mother and I were picking up the bill, as it were, for my father's crime. But . . .' He trailed off into silence again.

'But?'

'I don't think so. I remember getting a letter from him, knowing where he was in India, looking it up on a map, in my atlas, and wondering if . . . but then . . . then we lost touch. He moved. No one could track him down. And they hunted hard for him, believe me, because he was a suspect by then – a wanted, hunted man. They never found him, though. In the end we assumed he was dead.' A moment's reflection. 'My own private theory was that he'd thrown himself in the sea. He'd lost his daughter, whom he loved more than anyone in the world, and the grief was too much for him.'

Silence. The echoes of my own lost child, bloody, limp and dead as he slipped out of me, came wailing back.

'But now . . .' he said mysteriously, as though secure in some knowledge, some clue that he wouldn't reveal to me, 'I'm sure he didn't do it.'

'You don't think he did?'

'I know he didn't,' he said peremptorily.

'Right,' I replied, brought sharply out of myself by his decisiveness. 'So that's a little part of the mystery solved, then, is it?'

'Not that I was ever really in any doubt. But one's subjective view can be so blinding at times, can't it? Which is why it's so essential to keep talking it through. It was astonishing for me yesterday, for instance, to discover I'd never allowed for the possibility of an accident. Which is a perfect example of blind subjectivity. Or what a Buddhist would call karmic vision . . . narrow. Quite astonishing.'

I wasn't listening.

'Have I lost you?' he asked.

'I was thinking about your mother. You must hate her, don't you?'

I put this too bluntly, but I sensed that he preferred frankness to gentleness. He trusted it more.

'I can't seem to.' He said this as though it were a serious failing, as though it cost him more than he could tolerate. 'I wish I could, somehow. I'd be free of her then.'

4

I envied Kate. Well, there was plenty for anyone to envy about her. She had her own TV show as the country's first live therapist. She had a glorious home in Holland Park, she drove a gleaming new BMW, she was married to a successful and stunningly handsome man and, most enviably of all, perhaps, for me, she had two children, effortlessly born (and conceived). Should one of them not have been mine? At least one?

And yet, ironically, it wasn't any of these things that really hurt me any more. What I envied most about Kate by now was her ruthlesslness. Her ability to get her own way. To pick people up and put them down again without any remorse.

I realized as a child that, with this ability, she would outstrip me always, by a distance that I would never be able to cover as long as I lived. A literal analogy of our distinctly different personalities and the relationship between them was a race that I can remember running as girls – in which we stumbled over a lame dog that I stopped to nurse, while she flew on by like a bird. Winning, of course. She would always win. It wasn't that I couldn't run as fast, but I would always be held up by my heart. Somehow the more compassionate I was, the more heartless she became. And the more heartless she became, the more demonstratively (and remonstratively) compassionate I was.

Sometimes I wonder if there was only so much to go round between the two of us, and it was a question of who grabbed what first. Since she was born first, she grabbed everything she wanted just seconds before me, including her first breath, while I took what was left.

People used to speak highly of my 'kindness', because it served them well, because kindness serves everyone well. Except the kind. What they never saw was that I longed to be free of it. I longed not to care.

'Oh. Hi.'

She was cold.

'Can I come in?'

She walked away from me down the hall, leaving the door open. I was not welcome, but I could come in if I had to come in. Twins can read each other better without words.

'What do you want?'

Her abruptness was nothing new, but it still threw me.

'Er – well, I just wondered . . . I just wanted to ask you if –'

'I mean to drink. What do you want to drink?'

'Oh. Tea. Thanks.'

I paused.

'Why do I always feel that you're punishing me?'

'"Punishing" you!' she sneered. 'Is that a Person-Centred term?'

'You'll find it in any standard dictionary,' I said, trying to give as good as I got. 'If anyone should be punishing, it's me.'

'Why? What have I done?' she asked, laughing coquettishly.

'You tell me,' I said.

'God, you're pathetic, Mo. I'm a thirty-seven-year-old woman. Perhaps you still have time to "punish" people like some five-year-old, but having children of one's own makes that quite impossible.'

'Children and maturity in one,' I mumbled inadequately.

I saw myself in her as she spun round on me.

'What have you come here for?'

But I couldn't say.

'Because I haven't got time to be analysed by a heavy-handed, half-trained therapist just now.'

She poured the water from the kettle into the tea-pot, while I bit my lip.

'You have no idea what kind of therapist I am.'

'But we're about to find out, aren't we?' she said with forced good humour, filling the jug with milk and loading up the tray.

'What does that mean?'

'It means you've got a client who's a psychopath –'

'How do you know what kind of client I've got?' I demanded indignantly, wondering if Bill had already spoken to her, if they'd both been laughing about me.

'Howard North, as he calls himself. A psychopath. Everyone knows that.'

'Who told you I was seeing Howard North?' I watched the confidentiality clause slipping out of my grasp.

'I saw him, idiot. I know his car.'

I chose to deny it, if all she saw was his car.

'I don't know who you're talking about. Who's Howard North?'

'Bill seems to know who I mean.'

I felt the same old pang of jealousy. Had he come here this morning, then, when he'd stormed out of the house? Or was he here now, God forbid, hiding in some cupboard somewhere?

I followed her out of the kitchen and into the conservatory, my eyes looking everywhere for clues.

'Howard North is a very dangerous man,' she said. 'I'm really concerned about you.'

When had Kate ever been concerned about me?

'How well do you know him?'

'Well enough,' she said. 'You met him at my party, didn't you?'

'Lovely tea,' I said, resenting the fact that my new client was somehow hers too, that she could lay claim to him too, as well as everything else.

'He's a killer, Mo.' She was serious.

'What do you mean, he's a killer?' Was she deliberately trying to frighten me? 'What was he doing at your party, Kate, if he's a killer?'

'I didn't know he was a killer then,' she said, draining the blood from her face as if to order. A special effect.

'Who has he killed?' I asked, whitening a little myself.

'He killed his own sister, for one.'

Had he really? How much did she know?

'Tell me you're joking,' I said.

'I wish I was,' she said.

'How come he's a free man?'

'He was only a boy when it happened. And nobody's proved it. Yet.'

'Yet?'

'They're still trying to, especially – since his . . .' She stalled.

'Since his what?'

'Nothing,' she said. She was shaking.

'Are you all right?'

She ignored me.

'And he also drove a lover to suicide. Although I do wonder if it really was suicide . . .'

'How do you know all this?'

'I just do,' she said.

Did she? Or was she weaving a web of intricate lies and half-truths to wrap around me?

43

'Why do you wonder if it was really suicide?'

'I can't tell you,' she said. 'I can't tell you any more.'

I wasn't going to push when she had already said so much.

'Are there any others?' I asked.

'Not yet. As far as I know.'

I shuddered. I didn't entirely believe her, but I shuddered to convince her I did.

'You must feel weird,' I sympathized, feeling pretty weird myself. 'Was he a close friend of yours?'

'Very,' she said. The 'very' gave her away.

'Oh, Kate. How awful.'

'It is rather,' she said.

There was something hidden in the way she said this. I didn't know why, but at that moment I saw his lips meeting hers as if this had actually happened, and as if there was still something 'very' unresolved hidden in her heart. At least if this were true, perhaps it was Howard and not Bill that she loved.

There should have been relief in this, but there wasn't. In some curious way, Howard was becoming almost more important to me than Bill. Was it because he promised me some meagre success? While Bill and I had almost vowed to fail? Or was it just because he liked me? Because he needed me?

'Have you had a scene with him?' I asked her intrusively – but then she was always intrusive in my life, as if it were a right, somehow.

'Mo,' she said, like 'No' again, warning me. 'This tea's foul, isn't it?' she added, changing the subject.

'It's quite strange. What is it?'

'I don't know. Rose Poochong or something. Bloody Cliff. He never stops buying these awful brews. Have you seen the range of coffee beans we've got? It's like a bloody shop.'

She laughed almost hysterically. Really quite out of proportion to the joke, I felt.

'How is he these days?'

'God knows. I practically never see him.'

'Why not?'

'Too busy,' she said curtly, puncturing my curiosity. 'And Bill? How's he?'

'You tell me.'

'How should I know?'

'You see more of him than I do, Kate.'

She dismissed this as 'nonsense', and loaded up the tray.

But it wasn't nonsense. He spent far more time with her than he did with me. Whether they were actually screwing or not wasn't the point any more. The semantics were irrelevant. The point was that Bill and I didn't even feel married any more, we had grown so far apart.

In retrospect I can see that I had finally accepted this. I had stopped fighting for him. In some tacit, effortless way I had managed at last to let go. Which in turn (although he would never admit it) made him frightened to lose me.

'Have we sorted that, then?' she said.

'Have we?' I asked, unsure of what she meant.

'Leave well alone.' She meant Howard North.

She was so crisp and defined, Kate. Her therapy was a million miles from the anti-authoritarian ideals I cherished about my work. She always had to be in control, telling one hopelessly confused individual after another how to change their lives by subscribing to her view. Her will. But, oh, so charming, so charismatic, so clear. She made you believe in order, simplicity, sense. As if she could find a cure for every single problem you ever put to her. All you had to do was obey. If Howard had kissed her, it was his overpowering mother that he'd seen and desired in her.

'I've got to go,' she said.

5

Howard's next visit was a week later. I still hadn't seen Steph, nor anyone else that I could talk to with any candour. I'd left a message for my supervisor, but hadn't seen him either. I assured myself that as long as these two people were lined up for the future, all was well. One hour's supervision to four hours of client contact was the standard requirement for beginners. I was still 'ethical' – just.

His face was almost human again. The swelling in his lip had gone down substantially. The cuts and bruises had healed. I had forgotten quite how striking he was beneath that beaten face. Like carved marble. Eyes a steel-blue sky. Thick black hair painted grey at the sides, rolling back in waves from his broad forehead. A face you couldn't forget. Nor his body, which either stood like a statue, perfectly proportioned and still, or moved with an athlete's ease. There was grace in Howard North. A big man's grace.

I felt rather tatty in my old tweed suit. Not glamorous enough. I wanted to be very glamorous suddenly and to wipe the floor with Kate. I reminded myself that he sought my help because of who I was, because of something he wanted from me in particular, and that my physical image was not of great concern to him. But if Kate had won him, then I had to win him too.

He didn't greet me at all or even smile, but strode in through the front door as if it were his own territory. Purposefully.

'I shan't be coming next week,' he said as he sat down.

'Uh-huh.' I felt the pulse of failure in my blood. 'I'm sorry to hear that.'

His eyes stared intently ahead, straight through me, at some furious image far beyond me that I couldn't see.

'Is there any particular reason why?'

'Why what?' he snapped.

'Why you can't come next week?'

'Is that your business?' he demanded irritably, a palpable coldness in his eyes.

'Not if you don't want it to be.'

We sat in silence a while. A long while.

Eventually I asked, somewhat timidly, 'Are you angry with me?'

He looked at me as though noticing me for the first time.

'I don't particularly care for the female sex, if that's what you mean. And your precise colouring and features are more aggravating to me than any other combination of the two at this exact moment in time.'

He was a different man today. Rageful, tyrannizing, seething through my frailty like a hurricane.

'But don't take it personally,' he said.

'It's hard not to!' I tried to lighten the atmosphere, but the harder I tried the darker it grew.

'Have you ever been persecuted?' he asked.

'Aren't I being persecuted now?'

'Imagine yourself locked up in some metaphorical prison,' he said, ignoring me, 'and then someone turns up who tries to let you out – someone very particular tries to release you . . .'

'Uh-huh.'

'As this person is struggling to undo the lock, you both talk,

48

you laugh and cry together, you get to know each other and even to love each other, profoundly, in this time.'

'Uh-huh.'

'Then just as the lock is freed and you push open the heavy prison door, they thrust you back inside again. They betray you utterly. Everything you've ever told them about yourself in that intimate time when they were trying to release you is used against you now. You have no hope of escape. You are utterly lost. No one believes you. No one will ever try to release you again.'

Silence.

'Think about it,' he said.

I did. It was a torturous picture he'd painted, and it lived on in me.

'I may not be back the week after next, either. I may never be back.'

'I'm sorry. I'd hate not to see you again,' I said.

'Would you?' There was surprise and even tenderness in this first inquiry, but it was soon followed by a great outburst of rage.

To my astonishment, and perhaps to his own, too, he suddenly leapt to his feet and all but upturned my desk, pushing it violently towards me so that everything on it crashed to the floor.

I kicked the panic button with my foot until the alarm was screaming at us. He stopped in his tracks, a statue again.

'What the fuck do you think you're doing?' I said in half a voice as I left the room to switch off and reset the alarm. When I returned I found myself almost laughing I was so nervous.

'Jesus,' I said, shaking my head.

'I'm sorry,' he said.

'What were you doing?'

'Warning you,' he said, intensely.

'By turning my desk upside-down? Is that really necessary?'

He didn't answer.

'It's a very startling and aggressive thing to do, isn't it?'

'It's in proportion to the offence,' he said.

'What offence? I'm not even aware I committed an offence. What was the warning for?'

He didn't answer.

'Look, Howard, I made it clear to you very early on that I don't tolerate violence in my practice. Under any circumstances. I'm afraid I must ask you to leave.'

'That's interesting,' he said.

'I don't know if I'm willing to go on seeing you at all, in fact.'

'Heavens above! How on earth does anyone tolerate such a whimsical woman as you! You're married, aren't you?'

I didn't answer.

'You don't have children, do you?'

'Why do you ask?'

'I can't imagine them surviving you, that's why.'

'Please leave now. I won't allow this abuse in my practice.'

'There's that darling word again – impossible to escape it. Everything's abusive, Mo. You'll be shaking your impotent fists at the empty universe soon, crying out that death is abusive too, that social workers should put an end to it.'

'I'm sorry, Howard. If you don't go, I'll call the police.'

He looked genuinely nervous for a moment.

I got to my feet and reopened the door. Nervous or not, he kept me waiting there a good minute before he stood up. He was smiling. At the door he stood very close to me so that his breath caressed my cheek. I kept my eyes on the ground, waiting for him to pass me but he didn't move. He lifted my chin very gently until our eyes met. Then he smiled again.

'You're out of your depth, aren't you?'

That stayed with me, that sentence, for a number of reasons. First, because it was exactly how I felt. Second, because he seemed empowered by the fact and was evidently glad of it. And third, because little Cassie was out of her depth when she died.

Bill returned – from Kate's, I assumed – shortly after my session with North was through. As far as I could glean from either of them, they were co-writing a complex piece that was to run over several weeks, about paedophilia. It involved a great deal of research, so he spent hours in the library, poring over books from which he would select a short-list for Kate.

His work was creeping surreptitiously into my field and beyond, into the mind-bending world of analysis. Kate's world too, of course.

We were strangers; we avoided each other like reluctant lodgers in their own private worlds. Monosyllabic greetings were the best we could do.

I was in the hall, hovering redundantly, when he came home.

'Hi,' I said.

''llo.'

'Good day?'

'Not bad.'

Pause.

'Good.'

Pause.

'You?'

'OK.'

He made himself a cup of tea, my Bill, my big old tree, while I shut myself in my room.

If this was the end of my contract with North, it felt like the end of my life. Emptier now than it had ever been.

That night we lay still and apart on our backs, studying the crack in the ceiling. It was an ominous crack that we'd filled and refilled through the years, but it was beyond filling now, threatening to bring down the roof itself.

In the morning, with the sun up and glorious on a wealth of golden leaves, Bill still deep in sleep, unconscious as a corpse, I ached with a sudden longing for my childhood home.

I could see my father in my mind's eye, walking down the garden path to fetch the papers and milk. 'Dada!' I heard my early voice cry. Protector from all harm. Loved one. Dada. Man. Don't die. And I could see my mother too, wearing her old straw hat, taking his arm in hers as she breathed in the heavenly day. And I wanted to be there, back there, I wanted them both back, to keep the depth of them for ever in my life. The loss of them was still an unbearable agony.

And now Bill was dead, too. That's how it felt.

'What's the matter?'

He was awake now, squinting in the bright day.

'Nothing,' I said.

'We've got to do something about that crack,' he said.

'I miss Mum and Dad so much.'

He didn't say anything. What could he say? He had listened to my grief for so many years, as a penance almost, for his affair with Kate at that time. What could he say now, with the rift between us so deep and so wide?

'I seem to miss them more, not less, each year.'

'That's probably good, isn't it?' he offered half-heartedly. 'Means that by the time you die you'll probably have forgiven them for every petty harm they did. You might even stop competing with Kate for their love.'

He might have been talking about himself, with his harm done and my competition with Kate for his love.

'If she stops competing with me,' I said competitively. Why should I feel ashamed of minding what they'd done to me?

'I have to go to Wales today,' he said, throwing on a T-shirt through which his morning erection muscled for attention.

I watched him dress. How clumsy and lovable he was in his tousled, half-conscious fumblings. Zips, buttons, hair, even socks, all defying his best efforts to master them. I dozed off again, dreading full consciousness and all the dilemmas it would bring.

'See you, then.' Bill was standing by the bedroom door, looking down at me.

'Mmm?'

'I said see you, then. I'm off.'

'Oh. Right. Bye.'

But he stayed there.

'Bill? Are you OK?'

'This guy North,' he said, 'he's not your lover, is he?'

I almost laughed.

'Is he?' he demanded.

Good God. Was he jealous? After all these years of quiet indifference to me, was he finally jealous again? Jealous like he used to be, wildly, furiously? Or was he just curious to know?

And when I still didn't answer, he added that, frankly, he had understood it to be what Kate called 'unethical' to see a client without a supervisor, or a therapist.

'Without a The Rapist' he said, as if this joke hadn't been cracked with all the same cynicism before.

'Fuck Kate,' I said. 'Why can't you be as cynical about her?'

'Grow up, Mo.'

'And anyway,' I said, 'I'm seeing Steph today.'

'Well, good, I'm glad,' he said, but he was furious. 'Maybe she can persuade you that North is a psychopath. Nobody else seems to be able to.'

'Do you want me back after all?' I said.

'What?'

'As soon as somebody else might want me more?'

'I just don't want you hurt.'

'That's news,' was all I could manage as he walked out, the words seeming to echo in the hollow of the hall.

6

'What I'm picking up is that you're ... deeply involved with him in some way – intrigued by him? Drawn? That you can't – that you don't want to let go of him? But there's also something else ... there's a real fear of him – or of holding on to him? Of keeping him in your life?'

Steph always 'picked up' the truth, and never more incisively than she did then. I loved the way she felt around for the words, for the sense of what you were telling her, always questioning, never assuming a thing. Except that I did notice more of a statement than a question in 'there's a real fear ...'

Originally I had found Steph's method of working almost ridiculous. She verged on the mystical, as though convening with another world. A spiritual world? Perhaps she would claim that she was. Personally I'm fairly cynical about all that. Perhaps if I'd had a little more faith in something spiritual I might not have suffered such intense and ongoing fear, nor invited what I did. But we are who we are.

She was waiting for my response like an alert field-mouse, her beady eyes smiling at me patiently.

'Yes. That's it. That's exactly how I feel. Compulsively fascinated, as if I have to get to the bottom of it.'

'It?' she asked, but as if she was sharing the feeling somehow.

'I don't know what "it" is at all. It's like a sixth sense, as if there's some mystery, some secret I've got to get my hands on. It's like a challenge ...'

'And what I immediately think of, when you say a challenge, is Kate . . .'

'Kate?'

'We talked last time you came about her success, how it challenges you?'

I didn't want to talk about Kate.

'And I also think, when you speak of a sixth sense, of your husband . . .'

My husband. How strange the word seemed.

'Uh-huh.'

'You described – with some envy? – his instinct for a good story, his sixth sense?'

'Yes, I did, you're absolutely right.'

'Perhaps it was a projection of your own? Or –'

'Well, I – sorry – or?'

'Or is there a parallel here? Between Bill's investigative journalism and this curiosity you have about Mr North? As if – and this might be way off-beam – as if you're competing with Bill somehow, but you're in a different profession?'

'But, Steph, you have to admit there are many similarities.'

'Between the professions? Are there?'

I felt slightly ashamed then, as if my motives for choosing the profession I had were in some way unclean.

'And are those similarities what attracted you to this profession in the first place?'

'I feel as if I've done something wrong.'

'At this moment?'

'Mmm.'

'OK. Can you say more about that?'

She really did stay with me all the way. I thought of what I'd learnt in college, and of how ineffectually I put it into practice when I compared myself to Steph.

She was waiting again.

'As if you're shocked by my curiosity,' I said.

'OK. D'you want to know my real response?'

'Mmm.'

Not really, I thought.

'I'm not at all shocked. I was aware when I said "curiosity" that I was using my word. Your word was "fascination". And I was using my word because that's often what I feel in this job. Really curious!'

She laughed easily, quite at peace with this part of herself. I thought how interesting it was that with certain parts of ourselves we are perfectly at ease. We'd had a good look at them, they wielded no power, they were under our control. But there were other parts of ourselves which erupted from within like wild animals: uninvited, unwelcome, unknown. We became different people then. Awkward, shifty, ashamed. Frightened of ourselves.

'Are we travelling together still?' She beamed warmly at me.

'Yes.' I smiled.

'Where did you go?'

'I was just thinking about repression.'

'And I was thinking how repressed this area is for you – isn't it?'

'Which area?' I asked defensively. I'd forgotten how uncomfortable it could be on this side of the therapeutic exchange.

'This healthy curiosity you have, you seem quite – ashamed – of it?'

'Yes, I suppose I am.'

'Can you say more?'

'Like what?'

'In what way you're ashamed, or why, or . . . ?'

I was really uncomfortable then. I think I even blushed. I didn't want to say more.

'You seem very embarrassed, Mo.'

'Mmm . . .'

'Do you want to say what that's about?'

I let out a heavy sigh, which she mirrored.

'This whole area is still so . . .'

'So?'

She was unremitting in her efforts.

'So uncomfortable.'

'I can feel that,' she said, and she started wriggling around slightly in her skin. 'Feels tight in here, constraining . . .'

'Mmm . . .' I acknowledged the accuracy of her physical insight rather begrudgingly.

'Are you cross with me?' she asked pleasantly.

'Yes.'

'Thought so!' She smiled.

'I don't want to break new ground and I can feel you pushing me to.'

'OK. Let's leave be.'

She fell silent, which was very clever of her. She just left me with the door half-open on a whole powerhouse of feelings which might really help me. They might throw some light on North, or ease the tension with Bill, or possibly both. Unexplored, they promised miracles.

'D'you know, I think it's to do with sex?'

'Yep. That's what I think, too.'

How dare she, I thought. How dare she be so at ease with this dark secret in me?

'This man – Howard . . .' I began.

'He sounds like an attractive man . . .'

'Does he?' I pounced, greedily.

'Does that make it OK?'

'Make what OK?'

'That he sounds attractive to me. Does that make it OK for you to be attracted to him?'

I hadn't even admitted to myself the attraction I felt for North. Why should I admit it to her?

'Maybe,' was all I said.

She fell silent again, smiling kindly, encouragingly, determined not to push. I had the sense that she could see something I couldn't see, something I was blind to that everyone could see except me, a most intimate part of myself that I didn't even know was exposed.

'I'm supposed to be the good girl. Maybe that's it,' I said.

'Say more, if you can?'

'Kate's bad, I'm good. I'm not allowed to be bad.'

'So where does the badness go?'

'Lock and key, Steph! Repressed! Group 104 security!' I was trying to laugh at myself. I knew I could say more to Steph than to anyone else in my life about who I really was, but could I tell her what I hadn't even told myself?

'And the badness – what is it exactly?'

I could feel my heart sink through the earth, burying its secrets in the dark, enclosing soil.

'I don't know,' I said. Nor did I want to.

'Not just sex?'

'God, no.' I laughed. 'If only it was just sex!'

'If only it was just sex,' she repeated, so that I could hear the words, hear the admission I had made to something far more troubling.

'Can we talk about something else?' I said, uncomfortably.

'It's your hour, Mo.'

How I imitate her, I thought.

'I need to talk about Bill. Me and Bill. We're just so – I don't know ... We're so estranged.'

'OK.'

'It's not OK,' I said, exasperated by her glib, easygoing response. 'It's terrible, and it's my life. It's the whole of my once-happy life turned upside-down!'

'Your once-happy life?'

I felt that she wasn't with me any more, that she was outside me, looking in.

'Don't just sit there like the big I AM, Steph, as if you know what's best for me. You don't. You haven't got a clue.'

She smiled and nodded and tried to stay on my side. She was struggling.

'What are you trying not to say?' I asked. 'You might as well tell me.'

'What I'm thinking is, I don't have a memory of this happy life with Bill. I don't recall hearing about that.' She was puzzled, furrowing her brow.

Silence. Like the truth. Like a boulder in the middle of the room.

'Before we were married it was good.' But was even that true?

'Uh-huh. And when was that? Ten years ago?'

'I haven't forgiven him. That's what the real problem is. Ten years, and I still haven't let it go. It's my fault, Steph. And now I'm taking revenge.'

'Revenge?' She was surprised. 'Doesn't sound like revenge to me.'

'Doesn't it?'

'Sounds to me like you're getting some attention for once.' She watched me take this in. 'He respects you, Mr North, doesn't he? He values you.'

'But what do I do about it?' I pleaded, my panic audible.

'What do you want to do? Depends how attracted you are,' she said calmly.

'Or how frightened I am.'

'Or are you just frightened of yourself?'

I didn't think I was. I was genuinely frightened of something I could sense in him, but I didn't say so. Nor did I tell her anything that he'd told me about himself. I didn't want her to spot a danger so great that she would intervene in some way, abort my adventure before it had even begun.

'Perhaps that's all it is.' I nodded. 'I'm frightened of the feelings . . .'

'And they're just feelings,' she said.

7

For days afterwards I awoke each morning with a heady feeling of anticipation. Of what, I really didn't know. It was mixed in with a deep feeling of remorse, and neither feeling won the day. I felt pulled equally between the two. Perhaps I was anticipating midnight callers again. If I was, none came. The remorse was undeniably for Bill, but North was in there, too. I didn't hear from either of them and I didn't contact them. I didn't contact anyone. Every night I retired to bed restless, disappointed, and alone.

Then one day I woke up late, too late for either feeling to get the better of me, and hurried to be on with the day. I switched off the alarm, grabbed the post, and made myself a cup of coffee. I sank on to the sofa we had taken for ever to choose and missed Bill. His familiar ordinariness.

I flicked through the pile of letters and put the brown envelopes aside for later. A postcard from Bill's mother, as usual addressed only to him, from Malaga. She had bought a timeshare there and was always inviting him out to cover an ever-unfolding story about some expatriate. This card was no different. 'A big wet kiss from your loving Mum. XXX.' Mothers and their sons. An invitation from two close friends to their wedding anniversary, which somehow emphasized our own current separateness. And finally a letter written in handwriting both distinct and unfamiliar, an elegant swift run of black ink on a cheap white envelope. A London postmark.

Mo.

I was sorry to have frightened you. Truly. I seem to have been blessed with an alarming ability to terrify. Especially women. I had rather hoped you might be the exception. I do honour your decision not to see me again, but I wonder if you might agree just to meet me for a drink somewhere? Do telephone.

North.

The letter was so uncharacteristically polite. I thought of how effectively he had frightened me, and of how harmless he now seemed, if only because of this admission of his. His 'ability to terrify'. I even felt sorry for him. Perhaps this was his intention. If it was, it worked.

How could I trust my fear, my instinct for danger, when I had only recently witnessed a brutal murder in what had seemed to me to be harmless circumstances? In my efforts to identify reality I still doubted what reality was.

I telephoned. There was hardly time for it to ring before he answered.

'Yes?'

'Howard?'

'Speaking.'

'Mo.'

'Mo.'

And then a pause.

'Er – I got your letter . . .'

'Good.'

'Would you – well – where would you like to meet?'

He gave me elaborate directions for a place by the river overlooking Tower Bridge and then asked:

'Shall I pick you up?'

'Thanks. I'll make my own way there.'

Just in case, I thought.

We arranged to meet at six. At five, I soaked myself in a long, hot, scented bath. Exotic smells. There was the undeniable feeling of anticipation back again, bounding about inside me like an excitable dog. Thoughts of Bill came knocking at my heart but I locked the door on them.

I chose my clothes carefully. I thought they exhibited an easy naturalness, a wearing of the world like a loose garment round my limbs. But when I looked at myself in the mirror before I left, I saw restraint. A wildness hemmed in.

I found the place early and sat a while in my car. Tower Bridge glowed in the winter evening sun like a fairy-tale castle, a magical palace that didn't really exist, or that had shot up through the water like King Arthur's sword. Excalibur.

Howard was also early, I noticed. He stood with his back to me, gazing out at the same magnificent sight. Did it thrill him as it thrilled me?

I got out of the car at six o'clock and he turned instinctively towards me. He looked different, although the same elegance lent itself to his form. His whole presence seemed gentler, less forbidding.

'Hello,' was all I could manage. I felt shy of him now, in this different context.

He didn't reply but smiled, ushering me into the bar. He made his way determinedly to a table by the window and pulled out a chair for me.

'What will you have?'

'Apple juice? Anything soft.'

I watched him struggle with his impatience as he waited at the bar. When at last he returned I was so absorbed by the river-life, the boats, the nostalgia that these evoked in me, I didn't notice him.

'Mo.'

He was already sitting down opposite me.

'Oh. Thanks.' I gulped down the cold juice.

'Do you like boats?'

'They remind me of my father,' I said, and then wished I hadn't.

'Is he a sailor, then?'

'No. He just loved boats. He wanted to live on one.'

'Now that I can understand.'

I didn't want him to understand. I didn't want him to know anything about me. I wanted to go on being a mystery. Our previous relationship had allowed me that. Now, even with this small revelation, I felt the power run out of me like blood from my veins.

'I'm afraid this meeting really disqualifies our counsellor–client relationship,' I announced somewhat formally, retrieving a little control.

'Why?'

'It would be unethical to continue.'

'According to whom?'

He had a conceited smile on his face that implied a superior knowledge, but also a gentle teasing of my pomposity.

'Generally it's considered quite inappropriate,' I said.

I feared another outburst of his rage as I crossed him once more, but he remained calm and amiable, still half-laughing at me.

'What was your training? I've forgotten.'

I didn't believe he had forgotten. I remembered at Kate's party his enthusiasm for the man whose ideas I most admired, his delight at my admiration for their unconventionality, his constantly bringing the conversation back to my training and beliefs.

'Neville Hoare,' I reminded him.

'Of course. The man himself.'

Surely he was laughing at me?

'I'm surprised you've heard of him.'

'Why?'

'Few people have. Even fewer like him.'

'Is that so?' he said thoughtfully. He went quiet for a while. 'I don't know much about him. I've heard Kate mention him once or twice. He sounds quite unusual. Not your run-of-the-mill soul-saver, is he?'

But I didn't want to talk about a complex man like Hoare with someone who hardly knew his work. And anyway I was thinking of Kate, of her bruised, swollen, made-up, covered-up cheek.

'How do you know Kate?'

'Kate?'

'Have I asked the wrong question, Howard?'

'Can a question be wrong?' he asked rhetorically.

'A question can be compromising, can't it? Let's not play with words.'

He looked at me in silence for what seemed like an eternity. An untroubled grey-blue gaze. Or was he looking at Kate? A smile carved its way into his lips.

'You're extraordinarily beautiful,' he said.

My heart sank. This was a moment I had longed for and dreaded, both. In equal measure. It wasn't the flattery, but the intention behind it that so thrilled and daunted me. I looked away, out of the window at the boats. Dada and his boats. This infant in me, seeing so subjectively still what I might take from the world. Me, me, me. Nurture my baby soul. Mama, Dada, both. Love me all. Love no one but me all. Do not have eyes but for me. Bill. My Bill. Be man. Be Dada for me, father me so, and I will mother my son. Give me back my childhood better than it was and I will mother you.

'Have I said the wrong thing, Mo?'

I looked back at him. This stranger. This danger to me.

'Possibly.'

He took my hand and turned it over in his, toying with it like a cat with its prey.

'How tiny it is. Like a child's.'

I snatched my hand away and stood up, betraying my confusion and fear.

'I think I'd better go.'

'Very well.'

He kept his eyes trained on me, bewildered now, reluctant to lose me.

'You needn't fear me,' he said.

'Oh, really? You needn't be so frightening,' was my quick retort.

Pause.

'I expect that's true,' he conceded.

'It's difficult without rules to follow, isn't it?' I said, a little more kindly.

'Doesn't your guru disapprove of rules?'

'If you must know, he's not my guru. And, yes, in many ways that's quite true.'

He smiled.

'What's so funny?'

'Nothing. I'm interested. Go on.'

I didn't believe he was interested at all. I believed he wanted to watch me hold forth ridiculously so that he could patronize me.

'Basically, Hoare posits that rules are fundamental to identity, but only if some of them are broken. By choosing which rules to break, individuals define themselves. If the rules are good and true, they won't need to break them. It's only the repressive social rules he likes to see broken.'

'And our rules? Which are they?'

'Well – they're the ethical rules by which one abides as a counsellor.'

'One?'

'I. By which I abide.'

'Are they dictates, or are they rules you choose for yourself?'

'Both.'

'And ours?'

'Ours?'

Somehow 'ours' seemed excessively intimate.

'Yours and mine?'

'We've broken our rules already, Howard. You broke my rule by upturning my desk. I've broken another of my rules by meeting you socially. But one rule I won't break is to see you as a client again, having met you like this. It would be unethical.'

'Is that what Mr Hoare would say?'

'It's what I say. Neville Hoare isn't some god to be obeyed.'

'Is he still alive, this man?'

'I assume so. He still writes the occasional book.'

'You've not met him, I take it?'

'He's totally elusive. I don't know anyone who's met him. Makes you wonder, doesn't it? It could be a monster we're all studying.'

Howard smiled again.

'Sit down,' he said. 'Please? Just for a while.'

He took my hand and drew me back to my seat.

'I seem to keep upsetting you. I don't mean to, Mo. There's no one I'd rather please.'

I avoided his eyes, staring hard at my beer-mat. I kept

thinking of Bill, of our courtship, of how thrilling it had been.

What am I doing here?

I fitted the round base of my glass centrally on to the beer-mat. We do these things when there is nothing else we can do.

'I've had a difficult – unexpressed – life,' he said. 'I wanted to tell you. Tell you about it. The whole story.'

When I got home the lights were on and Bill's car was parked outside. I felt the keen edge of fresh deceit cutting into our lives. My deceit now, not his. His was something we already knew about, a part of the marriage that we had somehow contained. Or had we? Had we ever?

It was easier to be the victim, I realized, than to inflict the wound.

Our mutual deceit had now become a lethal blade, severing all communication between us, all heart-to-heart transfusion of the truth.

'Bill?'

The television was on. *Newsnight* was reporting crime statistics for the 1990s. There had been a decrease in burglaries but an increase in violent crime. As if we hadn't noticed the latter. Bill was asleep, his face squashed up against a cushion like a child's. He was always asleep, it seemed. Either away or asleep. For once, I felt relieved, and turned to go, anxious to deceive him further by changing out of my silk dress into something more demure. But he stirred and opened his eyes.

'Hi,' I said, braving his cold eyes. 'How was Wales?'

'Fine.'

He looked away, watching the television studiously. News was, after all, his subject, and had often been a useful focus when awkward emotions emerged. I watched it, too, perching on the end of the sofa.

'How can they say it's gone down?'

'What?'

'Burglary,' I explained, aware that he wasn't actually listening to the programme at all. 'I thought it was so popular now they were teaching it in schools.'

'They're manipulating the figures, that's all. What they don't say is that most of the crime is burglary-related. They just call it "violent crime" instead of "burglary" so it looks like they've got a result – in one department at least.'

'Oh, the deceits of this world . . .' I mused idiotically, asking for trouble.

'Tell me about them,' he said.

He said it like a world-weary journeyman whose last flicker of faith in human integrity has finally been blown out. Was it my flame? Or his?

I felt that my own deceit was rank, that he could smell it on me. Was I even deceiving myself? I had agreed to meet North 'as a friend' the following day. To hear this whole story of his. Whose 'friend' was I?

Bill switched off the sound with the remote control and looked at me. Finally.

'Where have you been?'

'Out.'

'Where?'

'To a pub.'

'Who with?'

'A friend.'

'Who?'

'No one you know.'

'Male or female?'

'Does it matter to you?'

'Male or female?'

70

'Male.'

'Who?'

'A friend, Bill. Just a friend.'

'Who? Friends have names, don't they?'

'I'm not going to have this conversation now.'

I got up to leave the room but he grabbed my arm and pulled me back down on to the sofa. He stood up and paced about in front of me, glaring at me wildly. I hated this side of him. Perhaps I should have been pleased that he cared, but it was too late for that. I didn't want him to care.

'You look very smart. For a pub. Best silk dress.'

'So?'

'Sure it wasn't dinner?'

'Yes, Bill, I'm sure it wasn't dinner.'

'First time I've known you to dress up for the pub.'

'There's a first time for everything, I guess.' Did he hear the irony?

'Howard, was it?'

'Who?'

'How is the dear psychopath?'

It was then that I noticed Howard's letter lying open on the table. I had left it there, of course, without the faintest notion that Bill would be back that night. He snatched it up and waved it under my nose.

'Heroic Howard North who rings your bell in the middle of the night. Literally, I mean. Only you can tell us if he rings it metaphorically, too.'

'Don't be ridiculous.'

'Oh? Is that ridiculous? Kate says –'

'Kate! Have you been talking to Kate about this?'

'Something wrong with that?'

I felt instinctively that there was something very wrong with

71

that, something far beyond their treachery, which I couldn't put my finger on. But I did my best to conceal this from Bill, making light of what I could.

'Not at all, Bill. Why should there be anything wrong with talking to Kate so intimately about me?'

'That was ten fucking years ago!'

Was jealousy all we had left to share? A petty possessiveness?

'I loved you, Bill,' I said.

'Kate says he's a very attractive man.'

'Kate married Cliff. If that's her idea of attractive, she's welcome to it.'

'Oh, come on, Mo. Everyone knows that Cliff is an incredibly good-looking man. He's practically famous for it!'

In fact this was true. But Cliff was Kate's, and anything of Kate's was becoming less and less attractive to me.

'I'm talking about personality, Bill, not face or physique.'

The argument was facile but inevitable. We would shortly have to discuss the merits or otherwise of Howard's physical attributes, both of us knowing full well that sexual charisma lay like a buried treasure, far beneath the surface level of skin.

'He's got personality, too, I hear,' Bill said.

'Well, honey, just for the record, he made such an impression on me the first time I met him, I couldn't remember what the fuck he looked like when he called.'

He laughed at this, at what he thought was yet another lie. In fact it was almost the first truth I had told.

'She says he's the archetypal hero of every woman's dreams. Would you agree with that? Just out of interest?'

What was she doing, feeding Bill's frightened imagination with images like these? Did she want to drive him frantically back to me? And if so, why?

'I've no idea,' I said.

72

His distress, such an unusual feeling for him to experience in relation to me, was fast turning into rage.

'Surely you would. You'd agree with Kate. You are twins, after all.'

'So?'

'Presumably you fancy the same men.'

'Why should we? We're not the same people, Bill. You should know that.'

'But the same men fancy both of you.'

Back came the cruelty. He could hurt me in spite of everything, and he revelled in it. I came up for air.

'I don't want to know, Bill.'

'But it's not news, is it? You've always known I fancy Kate. And that she fancies me. We were lovers, for God's sake!'

'Jesus, Bill . . .'

Did he mean me to feel that old panic again? The panic of losing him. The rush of jealousy, the urge to possess what I didn't even want any more. I had spent our entire married life trying to hold on to his love, when he had thrown it away at the very start.

'I must say, I don't blame you. We haven't made love in so many years, you must be crying out for it.'

'What about you? Aren't you, if I must be?' My voice was trembling.

'*What were you doing with him?*'

It was a sudden cry of pain, as if he could sense something far worse than ever I had forecast.

We stared at each other. It was one of those moments when you choose a direction that changes the whole of your life. Full of renewed feeling, full of compassion again, do you love and forgive, or do you draw the line? Do you volunteer for more pain, or do you say never again?

73

I chose to draw the line. But I kissed him full on the mouth, as if this could somehow wipe out the truth of what I had done.

He devoured my mouth as if it were food, a food he hadn't tasted in years. His hands groped at my breasts as if kneading dough, before clawing at the stockings beneath my dress, wrenching at them greedily so that they burnt my thighs, his fingers digging into me. He tore the offending dress from me so that it ripped at the seams. Then he threw me on the floor and penetrated me in almost every way that he could, before collapsing in a half-satisfied, half-tortured wail of relief.

He had raped me, effectively, since I'd had no will for it, since he had used such force. But I had surrendered, so . . . In a court of law they would say that I hadn't struggled enough. I could have hit him or screamed, but I feared more force still. And somewhere at the back of my mind I thought I deserved it. I even wanted the finality of it.

In the early hours of the morning I woke sweating feverishly, plagued by a recurring nightmare.

Ironically, although I was suffocating with heat, I had been dreaming of a terrible coldness, of living on a strange planet colder than any coldness I had known. Was it Europa, Jupiter's fourth moon? Frozen over like a cracked white eggshell, bleeding blue water from its wounds? Wherever it was, I couldn't ever grasp its laws. It seemed much like earth, in that it was peopled by the same human race, but every human instinct I possessed was alien to them and punishable by law. In vain I endeavoured to grasp the logic by which they lived so that I might belong to their world. I longed for their immunity to the cold.

It was killing me. Killing the warm heart of me.

I woke startled and ached with the loss of Bill. For ever a loss now.

When eventually he and I had climbed into bed, he had offered me his back, and I had offered him mine. And there would be no turning back.

8

I didn't sleep for the remainder of that night but lay staring at the crack in the ceiling until birdsong and first light. They brought rain. As I slipped quietly from our bed I felt the sharp edge of cold air. It was shocking to me, a hard, shuddering cold. November now. Winter was waiting for me, summer finally done.

I wandered downstairs at a distance from myself – a distance of both the head and the heart, as though watching myself on a screen, an unscrupulous anti-heroine for whom I felt only contempt. Perhaps if I had exercised some of the empathy then that Neville Hoare's teachings had always urged me to, things would have been different. Even before trying to forgive or understand Bill, I might have sat down with myself, reached out a hand, tried to understand where I'd strayed. But my empathy was all used up on North. I hadn't learnt to apply the same generosity to myself.

After a fresh coffee and two Cox's apples I stole back into the bedroom for clothes, any clothes, I no longer cared which. Bill stirred in his sleep as I opened the wardrobe door, and the sound stopped me short, as a healthy conscience might, but, once sure of his continued sleep, I crept away to dress. I wanted to be out of the house before he stirred again. It was still relatively early, only seven o'clock – my rendezvous with North was at nine – but I chose to leave then rather than risk a further confrontation with Bill. Sure that the sound of my car would rouse him, I pulled away fast enough to qualify for the Grand Prix. I dreaded the sight of his face at the window, his tousled crop of fair hair above his smooth skin creased by the restless sheets, his lips mouthing questions at me. I didn't look up.

I had two hours to kill. Or an hour and a half. The drive from Shepherd's Bush to the Isabella Plantation in Richmond Park would take half an hour at most on a Saturday morning.

I knew that Howard lived in Chiswick – he had given me his card at our first session – and I felt an overwhelming curiosity to see the house itself.

My heart was pounding in my chest as I turned down the road itself – a road full of fine Georgian houses, ablaze with burning-red Virginia creeper. A distinguished, wealthy air pervaded the comfortable half-asleep street. Each house was fronted by wrought-iron railings or high walls and gates, generous porches, handsome front doors in rich hues of green, blue, crimson and black, their brass accessories gleaming in the rain. And yet they conveyed somehow a contrived, sober modesty which served only to adorn their splendour further, like a thin veil over a face. Beauty is always best hidden. Flaunted, it courts enemies.

I thought of our plain old Shepherd's Bush house, dull and big as an over-large frock. How envious I felt of these elegant homes. How ashamed, too; how inadequate I felt that Howard had even seen our place. Had he anticipated something like Kate's place, at the very least?

I drove slowly down the road, searching for his house, his number, his home. It was easily the finest of them all. Exquisite as his tailored clothes. An immaculate old Mercedes lazed in the drive, a demure gun-metal grey.

I pressed down on the accelerator, terrified of being seen. I looked a mess. What could I offer him now, disempowered as I was? No magical skills to promise him, no therapist's role to play. Nakedly myself.

At the end of the road I discovered the river gliding easily by. I envied its complacence. In fact I envied everything then. I watched myself with loathing, wanting all that wasn't me. I stepped out of my car, unsteady on my feet, into the pouring rain, and took a deep breath. It was the cleanest London air I had breathed since a walk on Hampstead Heath in the spring, but a damp, cold air now, sweet-smelling as the sea. I longed for the sea, for the countryside by the sea to swaddle me in swathes of peaceful green.

I was drenched by the time I roused from my half-conscious reverie. It was already 8.30 when I heard a door slam shut. I saw Howard's Mercedes pull out of his drive and glide towards me, glide like the river, glide like the sky, a gliding gunmetal grey . . .

Then Howard's figure was towering over me, lifting me up from the pavement, carrying me to his car, sitting me on the front seat, my soaking body marking the leather upholstery. I had collapsed. I was shivering uncontrollably with the cold, or the fever, or the Plague. We rolled back into his drive, the Mercedes grumbling about its cargo, I felt sure. I could almost hear its low, refined drawl reprimanding North for his choice: of all the women you could have, this drowned rat of a thing . . . But as soon as the engine's quiet hum was switched off, the lazy beast was silent again. Hugo, I christened it privately. Over-privileged, over-indulged, under-extended. Indolent.

I was almost hallucinating, I realized.

'Can you walk?' asked Howard, opening my door.

'Of course I can walk,' I said, but I fell out of the car on to his gravel drive and had to suffer the indignity of being carried in.

*

When I returned to full consciousness I was sitting beside a roaring fire, wrapped in a green silk dressing-gown. Swathed in peaceful green. I had nothing on underneath. Howard was sitting opposite me, frowning slightly, staring hard at the fire. I half-expected a woman's presence to waft into the room, but none came.

'Feeling better?' he asked, without looking at me.

'Yes. Much. Thank you.' I paused. 'I mean – I wasn't aware of feeling worse, in fact. Although obviously I must've done.'

'You collapsed.'

'Yes.'

I paused again, trying to read the expression on his face.

'You were very cold.'

'Was I?'

I wondered just how cold. Surely he hadn't undressed me himself?

'How cold was I?' I ventured cautiously.

He smiled, plainly aware of my discomfort but offering no reassurance.

'Very cold indeed.'

I blushed, feeling suddenly very hot.

'Did you . . . ?'

I looked down at the silk dressing-gown tied neatly around my waist, the too-big swathe of green. He knew exactly what I was wondering, and seemed to enjoy my uncertainty.

'It was somewhat necessary,' he finally confessed, 'under the circumstances.'

An involuntary smile danced over his lips. He looked down at the thick Persian rug, but I could see him quite clearly struggling to wipe it from his face. When eventually he looked up again, a stony seriousness had taken its place.

'I do apologize.'

'Where are my clothes?' I demanded indignantly.

To my astonishment he had the audacity to smile yet again.

'I'm so sorry. You have every right to be angry –'

'I certainly do.'

'But you must understand that – in spite of my best intentions – it afforded me the greatest pleasure to . . .' His sentence trailed off, but his eyes stayed focused on me, speaking volumes of their own. 'I must say, you do have quite the most beautiful . . . the most beautiful . . .'

He was frowning again, just slightly, as though discussing a work of art, not quite sure whether it really was so fine after all, and if it was, then what exactly it was that made it so exceptional.

'How dare you?' was all I could say.

He looked away at the fire, his glowing face suddenly sad, as though some thought or memory had swept him away from me. A great distance stretched between us.

'Your clothes are in the laundry-room,' he said dismissively, his voice suddenly cold – hostile, indifferent.

I think I was expected to leave then, quietly and graciously, like some meek, obedient slave, understanding, as no one else could, her master's troubled temperament. I stayed.

He continued to ignore me, surrendering wholly to his thoughts, which excluded me utterly.

It was this habit of withdrawing from me, I later realized, that made me determined to draw him out. His sudden stubborn silences created an urgent longing in me to hear this story of his, this whole account of his life.

'Howard?'

He seemed startled by the sound of my voice and, looking up, was plainly amazed to find me still there.

'What are you thinking about?'

He didn't answer, but looked away again at the fire. I thought back to our first session together, to his sister's 'funny little line' and his own 'curiosity'. I was wondering uncomfortably what pleasure my unconscious naked body had in fact afforded him when suddenly he got up from his throne of a chair and left the room.

I looked around me for some clue to the mystery he was. The room was heavy with atmosphere, panelled from floor to ceiling in wood. There were large, incongruously modern paintings on the walls. The thick lined curtains of eggshell blue exuded a musty-sweet smell. I studied the books on the shelves behind me, many of them classics, bound in old red or green leather. One shelf alone – the lowest – was confined to modern writing, paperbacks and hardbacks alike. It was crammed with books, in fact, as though struggling to contend with the weight of history above. To my astonishment, many of these books were modern psychology books. But more astonishing still, since he had denied even a nodding acquaintance with the man's work, he had every book of Neville Hoare's. Admittedly their spines looked untroubled by exercise.

Maybe he's only recently bought them all, I speculated.

I was about to pick one from the shelf and look at it when I felt the soft impact of flying clothes at my back. I turned round to see Howard, who had presumably thrown them at me.

'They're more or less dry,' he said.

'Thank you,' was my more or less dry reply.

'I must ask you to leave now,' he said.

'Sure.' I picked up my clothes. 'Tell me. Why the sudden change of mood?'

'Please get dressed. This is too familiar,' he said.

'I didn't ask you to take off my clothes,' I retorted.

'I don't mean familiar in that sense of the word.'

He turned his back to me sharply, looking out of the window at his gleaming car. I climbed discreetly into my underwear and then into my overwear until I was fully dressed.

'Shall I see myself out?'

He turned round suddenly, surprise and confusion blatant on his face.

'Don't go yet,' he said. It was an order, not a request.

'I find I'm happier with consistency, Howard – you know? I like a person to say something and stick with it – at least for a minute or two.'

'Sit down,' he said, plainly unamused.

Although the masochist in me enjoyed his domination, the freedom-fighter did not. Went to war, in fact.

'I'm so sorry, I didn't quite hear what you said.'

'I said, sit down.'

He hadn't sensed the edge in my voice. I persevered.

'Yes, I thought you said "sit down". My ears attempted to transmit the words to my brain, but there was something in your tone which my brain didn't recognize – hold on – I'm getting the message through now . . . it's just processing . . .' I paused dramatically, as if listening to my brain, and then said, *sotto voce*: 'Ah. I see. That's why . . .' before readdressing him. 'Apparently the tone you used was quite archaic – no longer in common usage – something to do with male domination? Tyrannical bullying? Make any sense?'

'Very good,' he said drily. 'You've come a long way.'

Absurdly, I was flattered. But I found the statement disarmingly patronizing too.

'Not literally, of course – you haven't actually covered any distance. You're merely treading water. But that's better than nothing, isn't it? When you're out of your depth.'

I thought of her again. Tiny dead weight in his hands. Or hers.

'What makes you think I'm out of my depth?'

'Aren't you?'

'What depths are they, Howard? If you could give me some indication of how deep I'm in, I might be able to say.'

He studied my face, examining its dimensions thoroughly, cocking his head to one side to get a fresh perspective on it.

'The likeness is remarkable,' he said.

I always hated these comparisons, common as they were.

'Can you imagine being a twin, Howard? How frustrating it is?'

He put his head straight again guiltily.

'Not easily,' he confessed.

'Imagine if people were always making assumptions about you because of how you looked, because of what they knew about your twin, because they'd screwed her or –?'

'I wouldn't like it at all.'

I felt that he was trying to cut me off somehow, to stop me explaining further, but I wanted to drive the point home. I wanted to see what he would betray of his intimacy with Kate.

'People I've never even met – men particularly – behave as if they have an intimate knowledge of me, simply because they've slept with Kate. Men I wouldn't even look at, let alone sleep with.'

He was silent. Intensely so.

'And since she sleeps with a different man almost every week, it makes life rather difficult for me.'

Pause.

'Does she?'

'Does she what?' I asked.

'Sleep with a – so many men?'

'Well, she's never been one to tire of it, put it that way. She enjoys her power too much. Even in her work. I expect she'd call it all work, mind you. Research or experimentation or something. She is a sex therapist, after all. Amongst other things.'

I said all this in a very matter-of-fact way, which indeed it was, but he looked decidedly uncomfortable.

'I've often wondered what would happen if her power failed her . . .'

'Her sexual power, you mean?' he asked, too urgently.

'She assumes she can conquer everyone who comes to see her – she would say "cure", but generally she cures by conquering, it's the conquest that motivates her –'

'How do you know what motivates her?' he demanded furiously.

'Because she's explained it to me,' I said. 'Am I upsetting you?'

'Not at all,' came the swift, suddenly calm reply. 'I can't abide assumptions, that's all. You seemed to be guilty of the very thing you were criticizing in others – namely that because you're twins, you must be alike.'

'We couldn't be more different,' I said, in my defence.

He fell silent.

I wondered whether I should leave, whether I had far outstayed my welcome there, but he scarcely seemed aware of me, so deep in thought was he. Then having said nothing for at least ten minutes, he offered me a coffee.

'Thank you.'

When he was out of the room I looked at his books again. He even had *Beyond the Law* – Hoare's most recent work. I still hadn't finished it myself. I flicked through its pages, hoping it would fall open at a passage that would change my life, that would reveal the world to me as I longed for it to be. Uncannily, it fell open on a chapter about sex. 'In this particular domain,' it read, 'the law-makers are the law-breaker's victims, since only they know what price they have had to pay.' I didn't get any further before he returned with a tray.

'Any you don't recognize?' he asked.

'Of . . . ? Oh – you mean the books?'

'I do indeed mean the books.' He poured the coffee.

'I certainly know all of Hoare's work,' I said, and couldn't resist adding, 'I thought you didn't know much about him?'

'I don't,' he said soberly. 'Honestly. If only I did.'

'But you've got everything he's ever written!'

'Do you know much about him from what he's written, Kate?'

'Mo.'

'I do apologize,' he said, immediately contrite. 'Mo.'

'Yes, I feel I do know something of him from his work.'

'What do you think you know?' He passed me a cup.

'I know he's an honest thinker,' I said devoutly. 'Thorough. He shines a light in the darkest corners of the soul.'

'Goodness.'

'He goes where no one has dared.'

'Brave, then?' he mocked. 'Honest and brave!'

'Very brave,' I answered gravely, resisting his ridicule. 'But I imagine he must be very lonely, too.'

'Why lonely?' He seemed suddenly disconcerted by this.

'Because he makes people so uncomfortable.'

'Ah. Indeed.'

'People like to be told life is simple and everyone is good.'

'Do they, Mo?'

'Whereas he tells them they're not good. Quite categorically. He tells them life is complex. Not simple at all.'

'Which, undeniably, it is. Complex, I mean.'

'But you'd be surprised how many people would rather think they were stupid or confused than admit that life is complex and difficult.'

We sipped our coffee thoughtfully.

'Do you really think that's true?' he finally asked.

'Yes.'

'Does Kate deny complexity, too?'

'Possibly,' I said, wondering why we were back with Kate. 'She's very single-minded. She doesn't like paradox, or complexity. You can see that in her TV shows. She believes in straightforward answers. Solutions. God help her if she ever meets with the truth!'

'Don't you believe in solutions?'

'Yes, of course. But it's always better to face unpalatable truths than deny them, isn't it?'

'Is it?'

'What's that line of Hoare's? "If you deny it, you are immobilized, if you admit it, you are resourced."'

'What a trite little saying!' He cringed.

'I don't think it's trite.'

'Of course it's trite. Anyone can write that crap.' He spat the words contemptuously.

'I think it's very profound.'

'Unadulterated faeces, Mo.'

His sudden mood swing left me bewildered. He was like two people, one cultured and civilized, the other thriving on anarchy.

I dug in my heels, determined not to lose myself.

'I don't agree. I think Hoare is immensely courageous. Wise and —'

'How can that kind of simplistic rationalizing be "wise"?' He cut me off abruptly, almost shouting at me. 'For all his tribute to complexity, how does a comment like that take into account all, or any, of the complexities we struggle with every day?'

'His writings are as capable as anyone else's of addressing life's complex entirety.' I was fierce in my defence of this great man, this hero of mine. 'He addresses life's whole better than anyone I know.'

'Life's hole?' echoed Howard, making a circle of his forefinger and thumb.

I moved towards the door, but he grabbed me.

'Don't be such a ridiculous, sentimental cow.'

He was holding me by the shoulders, his face furious and betrayed in mine.

'Use your fucking brain,' he said desperately. 'I need your intelligence, Mo, not your sentimental fairy-tales.'

'How is what I've said sentimental? I don't see it.'

'You're obviously in love with this bloody Neville Hoare. That's sentimental, isn't it? He can do no wrong in your eyes.'

'I'm sure he can do wrong.'

'Think for yourself, Mo. Don't think through books you've read by anonymous guru-men. I need you to think for yourself.'

Hugo the Mercedes grumbled slightly with old age as the accelerator was pressed down.

In Richmond Park we left him lined up with his inferiors, before setting off for the Plantation in wellington boots and coats. I was wearing an old oilskin which Howard had found buried in his cloakroom under countless jackets. It reminded me of a coat that Kate used to wear, the glossy black against her dyed yellow hair.

'Whose was this?' I asked, fingering the worn creases in the arms.

'No idea.'

He stood still for a moment, breathing in the damp, leafy air as if it were the scent of God. In that instant he seemed to transcend himself. And when he exhaled, a heaviness seemed to expel itself from his limbs.

'Ah.'

I fell in love with him then. I believe there is always a precise moment in love when we suddenly recognize the other person's soul, like an old photograph we know profoundly well, that for some reason we've kept and at last understand why.

He beamed with pleasure.

'Isn't it lovely?'

I nodded, hopelessly tongue-tied.

'I'm glad you're here,' he said easily, as if it cost him nothing.

'I am too,' I said clumsily, because it cost me everything I had.

We walked on in silence. I felt as though we were new lovers, too full up for words, bursting with the sweetness of life.

But, in concluding some long process of thought, he suddenly said:

'Women are the lovers, aren't they?'

And at once I felt found out, left out, guiltily alone with this new passion burning in my heart.

'What about men?'

'Women are the choosers. They hold everything together or rip it asunder with love. Love they choose to give or withhold. Women have the ultimate power.'

I was baffled by this out-of-the-blue generalization, which swept aside my whole experience.

'Are men only women's victims, then? Can they do no wrong themselves?'

'It's not a question of right or wrong,' he said impatiently.

'It's a question of the truth. It's beyond morality, thank God.'

The irony of this juxtaposition of concepts made me laugh.

'What's so funny?'

'Nothing,' I said, contrite. 'So whose fault is what, then? Or do you blame women for the lot?'

'You're looking for good and bad, Mo. The old morality. It's nobody's fault. There's no one to punish. It just is. The truth.'

We walked on in silence again. What experience had forced this conclusion on him, I wondered. Or was he right? Was it really as simple as that?

'Tell me about yourself,' I said.

The invitation was perhaps too general. He remained silent and thoughtful, as though waiting for the next, more particular question.

'Tell me about your mother, then,' I said.

'What about her?'

'Her story. Before – before the . . .' I couldn't say the words. The dead little face, eyes open, was staring up at me from my own arms, the luminous blue eyes like the tramp's eyes in Bloomsbury, the same beautiful face, only fresh and round and young.

'Before the drowning,' he said.

'Yes. Before the . . .'

He waited to see if I could say it now, but I still couldn't.

'My mother, then,' he began, pausing to collect his thoughts. 'She was born in India to a tea-planter and his wife. Darjeeling tea, it was. She was . . . heavenly. Is the word. I've seen photographs. A most beautiful child . . .'

He digressed dreamily into his own memories.

'But she was mostly ignored,' he resumed. '"Starved of attention" would be an accurate description. Her father was drunk all the time, or out chasing other women, while her mother was forever resting. Resting! I love the lies they told! Presumably she was in fact trying to cope emotionally with her husband's infidelities, and his drunkenness.'

We passed through the big iron gates of the Isabella Plantation. I had only visited it in the late spring, for the cool pinks, crimsons and whites of the camellias and the rhododendrons, but now the trees had their own glory, a dying chaos of oranges, yellows and reds.

'Needless to say,' he continued keenly, 'she grew up to be a beautiful woman. An exquisite beauty. She dazzled Calcutta. All those hungry British men, dreaming of a white woman's breasts and ... "Stiff upper lips, stiffer lower dicks" ...'

He laughed at his own little joke.

'Ever heard that one before?'

'No,' I said, embarrassed by his sudden crudeness.

I kept my own thoughts to myself. They were unclear, anyway. Mothers, breasts, mother's milk, sex, and finally Howard's dick. I should have been a Freudian ...

'My mother was allowed to be desired, you see. She was white. The British could openly worship her. It must have been tough for the whores, who were used to being preferred by the British. The Indians themselves treated their whores with utter contempt, since an Indian whore was living evidence of their own inferiority, but the British romanticized those whores.'

'Poor whores,' I said, 'passed to and fro ...'

'Indeed,' he said. 'But imagine the desire my mother kindled then – in the Indians and the British alike – rich and beautiful as she was. A perfect woman, even amongst her own kind. I can't think of a woman who could equal her ...'

High praise indeed. Too high. There was something odd

about it. I thought of his earlier admiration of my own modest beauty – of my face, on the first occasion, and of some other region that he had come upon that morning, on the second.

'She soon learnt to steal the attention of every man from every other woman in the room. That was her career, if you like. Securing the devotion of men. She was very good at it. She acquired a lifelong taste for it. If she didn't have a man's total devotion, she'd go to any lengths to secure it.'

He paused. His voice was less excited now, sober and dull.

'When she married my father, however, it was his devotion alone that she sought. Primarily because it was unattainable. Unfortunately for her, and for him – for all of us, in fact – she could never secure even a fraction of his devotion. He simply loved someone else. But because she was Indian, he couldn't marry her. That was the social unacceptability of the day.'

'How sad,' I said.

'So my mother married him instead. Of all the men to choose! She chose a man as unavailable to her as her father had always been.'

I thought of my own father, endlessly absent from my life. Was Bill his substitute, always away working somewhere?

'I could go back through each generation and show you how the patterns repeat themselves tirelessly. Even down to me. "Consciousness cracks the Code," as Neville Hoare would say. But I haven't noticed it.'

He was quiet now, falling into the inexpressible grief that swallowed up the air.

'I feel for you,' I said.

It was the wrong thing to say. He stared at me blankly, stranger that I was, an intruder suddenly in his private, painful world, where the past and the present – and doubtless the future, too – were woven like a net around him.

'Don't pity me,' he spat contemptuously. 'Just let me tell my story. From start to finish. I don't need your bits and pieces thrown in. Everything has a beginning and end, an action and reaction, a cause and effect. You have to see the whole.'

'It's OK. I'm listening,' I said. 'I'm trying to see the whole.'

'Use your head, Mo, not your heart.'

'My heart rules my head,' I said. 'I'm not here because you're an intellectual challenge to me, Howard. I feel for you.'

He looked truly horrified by this, almost disgusted. Everything about him hardened. I could feel the chill paralyse me. I wanted to say that I was confused by him, that I hated his abrupt changes of mood, that he was frightening me again, but I couldn't persuade my brain to move my lips. It knew better than I did that Howard North was two different men. One I now loved, the other I feared.

He walked on again slowly, safe in the knowledge that he could tyrannize me into submission whenever he wanted to. Or so it seemed to me.

I wondered how Bill was. My once-beloved Bill, now a cold stranger to me. He seemed so far away. On another planet, almost. In spite of myself, I missed him. However hollow our marriage had been, I missed the known quantity it was. The familiarity. But I relished the new, too. It seems that the mind craves change as the belly craves food, or it will atrophy. And if it cannot discipline itself to value as new what is old and familiar and worn, then it will seek novelty. Shots of adrenalin. Like a drug. Ultimately violent.

'I need you, Mo.'

It seemed to come from nowhere, unless a statue has needs. But he had moved up close behind me and I could feel his breath on my neck. I turned, and was met by his smile, the lips soft and open now, inviting me in.

The rain was pouring over us like honey, heavy and sweet.

'I want you,' I said.

'Now, Mo –' but I stopped his mouth, and his lips covered me.

Now, yes, I will have you. Take you. Admit you. Find, if you will, the deep entrance in. Under the evergreen glossy-leaved camellia tree. Penetrate me.

But that wasn't what he meant. He meant, 'Now, Mo, I will tease your desire.'

He brushed my cheek with the back of his hand, stroking it softly up and down, up and down like love. I longed for that hand to be seized by the same rapacious hunger I felt for him, but it teased on, while my senses frenzied themselves. Did I dare to make the first tentative move? To reach out, touch him, stir his desire? Find out what spoke to him there?

'Are you happy?' he asked.

'I love the rain,' I said.

'We're fairly drenched, aren't we?' He smiled. 'Let's go back.'

And back was what he meant. All the way back through his life. He took my hand and led me away. Led me astray. I let him. I had surrendered by then. He could lead me anywhere. Wet as a drowned babe.

9

I suppose, in effect, that he kidnapped me. It didn't feel like it at the time, but he never asked if he could drive me to the West Country. Not that I minded or had anywhere else to go.

'I was adopted, you know. I'm not my mother's natural child,' he announced, somewhere near Salisbury cathedral with its head in the clouds. 'No blood between us.'

I assumed he was denying the murderous blood, not any blood spilt.

'Where are we going, Howard?'

'Home.'

'Whose home?'

'Did you hear what I said?'

'You're adopted, yes.' But I hadn't really taken it in. 'Are you?'

'Cassie wasn't. But I was, for some reason.'

'But you were older than her –'

'That's right,' he said, in the same clipped tone he used to close most sentences he didn't want opened again. As one closes the lock on a full suitcase. Click.

'So she suddenly became fertile, your mother, or . . . ?'

He didn't reply.

'Howard?'

'I've no idea. It's anyone's guess. Perhaps they didn't have a – didn't enjoy a full . . . It's possible that they didn't – or couldn't – consummate the marriage until much later, is what I'm trying to say.'

Why does it cost you so much?

'That would be unusual,' I said. 'I mean – it's an odd way round, isn't it? Usually it's the other –'

'Yes.' He cut me off. 'As I say, I don't know.'

I wasn't going to leave it there, even if he was.

'Maybe with his Indian lover still haunting him, he couldn't – you know – sort of keep it – up. With your mother. So to speak.'

I was suddenly blushing absurdly, infected by his own dis-ease.

'As I said, anyone's guess.' He had the same click in his voice.

'Did he resent her terribly?' I asked.

'How on earth should I know? He left when I was five.'

'Didn't you ever see him again?'

He was silent, not to be drawn.

We pulled up, soon after, beside a large old family house with its own long drive. Georgian, again. Graceful, simple, clear. The sort of house that can look you straight in the eye with no secrets to hide. But, oh, how misleading those first impressions can be.

'So this is home? Your country seat, or . . . ?'

'This is where I grew up,' he said.

I took a deep breath.

'Right.'

'And where my sister was drowned.'

An ominous feeling crept over me. The excavation into his past had only just begun, I could feel that now. I sensed that he was pacing himself, like a runner, for the long distance ahead, while I was merely limbering up for a jog.

'Funny old place,' he said.

'Beautiful, isn't it?'

He was thoughtful. 'I haven't spent any time here, really, over the last two years. I came down to find my mother, that was all. About six months ago.'

'To find her?'

'Well, to look for her. I needed to talk something through.'

'Does she still live here, then?'

'My mother?' he asked, amazed. 'My mother's dead.'

Good God, I thought. Why is that such a shock?

'I'm so sorry,' I said. 'I didn't realize.' Pause. 'She must've died very recently?'

'Very recently.'

'For some reason I thought she was . . . still alive.'

'No. As it turns out. She's not.'

There was a perplexing fury in his voice, as if the audacity of her death had enraged him. Or something about it had. Something that was far beyond grief had deeply troubled him.

'I'm sorry,' I said again, feeling that it was somehow my fault.

He got out of the car and stood looking at the house for some time. I felt that if I got out of the car too, we would be there for days, weeks, possibly, so I stayed where I was until he opened the door for me and took my hand. We stood looking at the house together, my hand wrapped up in his like a lucky charm.

'I can't tell you how sick it makes me feel.'

'Sick?' I had been admiring the graciousness of the place. 'Why does it make you feel sick?'

'Can't you sense it? An overwhelming toxicity? Like chemical warfare. Gas.'

'A kind of malevolence?'

'Exactly.'

I could sense something, in fact, but I wasn't sure if it was coming from the place or from Howard. What I sensed precisely was not malevolence but despair.

'How long did you live here?'

'For as long as I can remember.'

'When did you leave?'

'I didn't.'

Could he mean that?

'I don't understand . . .' I said. 'You never left home?'

'No. Why? I lived here for . . . let me think . . . forty-six years? Yes, that's right. I'm forty-eight now.'

'Gosh,' I said, for want of a better word to express the astonishment I felt.

'Two years ago, I bought the house in Chiswick, so, if you like, I left two years ago, but . . .' he trailed off.

'But . . . ?'

'It wasn't a formal thing, ever. I just – didn't come back.'

He spoke of the situation as though it was relatively normal. A little unhealthy, perhaps, to an outsider, but nothing at all serious. If anything was serious, it was the fact that he 'just – didn't come back'. That was the thing that had been wrong. Leaving Mother had been wrong.

'So you left without telling her?'

'And without telling myself, more to the point. I just walked out. I packed a suitcase and walked. It was a late summer afternoon – Kittie was asleep on the sofa –'

'Kittie?'

'Katherine. My mother. Kathy, Kittie, Kate . . .'

'Kate?' I repeated, uncomfortably reminded of his intimacy with my twin.

'Occasionally, yes. Kate.'

'A strange coincidence?'

But he wouldn't be drawn.

'When did you first meet her?'

'Who?'

'My sister. Kate.'

'Mo. Behave yourself.' He smiled, pinching my cheek affectionately. 'It's not your business to interrogate me.'

'It's not your business to pinch my cheek,' I said.

For a moment he seemed delighted with me, smiling at me just long enough for me to feel quite shy.

'How beautiful you are,' he said.

I looked away. The Wiltshire landscape with its generous rolling hills lay like an indolent cat, hiding its feline teeth and claws in soft lolling lines. I felt his hand on the nape of my neck, caressing me gently, sending a fierce charge through the whole of me.

'Please, Howard –'

But he stopped my mouth with a kiss like no kiss I'd ever known. Perhaps because it was so unexpected? Exotic as an unfamiliar fruit. Soft. Moist. Extraordinarily sweet. Then he fixed his eyes on me again, as though sharpening the focus of a lens, before pulling away.

We stood in silence; the current between us seemed so strong to me now that it was almost tangible. I felt the dull ache of longing in my limbs, like pain. But he seemed immune to it. He was looking at the house again, as if the house itself had stirred the desire in him, as if I just happened to be there. There, but dispensable.

'Do you want to come in?'

'Sure.'

He took my hand once more and led me to the peeling black

front door. I presumed that he would unlock the door himself, but instead he rang the bell.

'Who lives here now?'

'I'm – renting it out,' he said, unconvincingly. 'This old boy – he was homeless and ... He's nutty as a fruitcake. You'll see.'

We waited an age for the old boy to answer the door. His white head of hair appeared first, as though charging at us. In fact he was charging after a cat that had just leapt out of his arms and was running through my legs. He straightened up, defeated by the chase.

'Kitty!' he shouted, presumably after the cat, although this wasn't entirely clear, since he was staring straight at Howard.

'Kittie?' Howard looked horrified.

'Hello, there, Mr North. I told her you'd be back. Kitty!'

'Told who?'

'Kitty!' he shouted for the third time.

'I think he means the cat,' I whispered as quietly as I could.

The old man bent down to retrieve the marmalade cat that had been the cause of so much confusion already.

'I do indeed mean the cat,' he said, straightening again and smiling politely – but icily – at me. 'How are you, madam?'

'Mo,' I corrected him. 'I'm fine, thank you. How are you?'

Confused, he smiled and nodded vigorously and said, 'Yes yes!' but wouldn't shake the hand I extended to him. Nor did he suggest a name for himself.

'Whose cat is it?' asked Howard, irritably.

'Whose are you?' was the old boy's reply.

'I'm sorry?'

'Who do you belong to, Mr North?'

'It's a heavenly beast,' I interrupted amiably, stroking its purring back.

'Do they have beasts in heaven?' he inquired.

I was getting the impression, pretty fast, that the old boy didn't like me very much, and that he liked Howard even less.

'Look, can we come in, just quickly? I don't want to invade your privacy or anything but . . .'

The old boy waited for Howard to hang his sentence clumsily in the air, unfinished, like half a car off a cliff. He left him suspended there for some time before rescuing him.

'My house is your house,' he said finally, which was obviously more of a fact than a hospitable gesture. 'Come and go as you please.'

Howard was climbing the stairs when the old boy grabbed my arm and whispered, terrified, in my ear:

'I can't find it anywhere. I swear.'

What on earth was he talking about?

Howard glanced back at us, frowning slightly.

'Is he bothering you?'

'Not at all,' I answered pleasantly, keen to investigate at my own leisure.

'Are you suggesting that I am harassing her?' asked the old boy indignantly, winking conspiratorially at me.

'Do come on up, Mo. I want to show you around.'

'Is she *another* woman, then? I understood you were married, Mr North?'

Howard didn't answer this rather intriguing question, but instead said:

'Please don't feel obliged to follow us about, sir. We shan't be long.'

The old boy stared up at him reproachfully from the bottom of the stairs like a banished child.

'Very well, very well . . .' he mumbled, withdrawing obediently.

Howard walked me straight into his mother's bedroom. He was clearly profoundly disturbed by the place.

'Nice view,' I said.

The view looked out over the garden at the back, a hopelessly overgrown tangle of climbing roses and broken pergolas, but the sweep of the hills behind was stunning.

'It's beautiful,' I said.

'Yes,' he muttered, his troubled gaze finding its way to the window. 'Yes, it certainly used to be. Katherine had a real feel for the garden. The colours – well you can hardly see them now – they were still flowering a couple of months ago, but – well, they complement each other so well.'

I was looking for water. Even a small boggy puddle would have sufficed to convince me that this had been the place. But I couldn't see it anywhere.

'It was filled in after the – after Cassie's death. It's overgrown now.'

'The pond, you mean?'

'Isn't that what you're looking for?'

'Yes.' I felt guilty, caught out. 'Where exactly was it?'

'Over there.' He pointed to the far left-hand corner of the garden. 'It used to catch the light from this room so vividly, gleaming like a silver coin. It was as if Cass was trying to haunt us. So Kittie filled it in.'

There was a long pause, which I left because I didn't know quite how to ask my next question, and which he left because he was haunted still.

'What actually – happened to her – I mean to her body? Once she was dead?'

He looked so frightened.

'I don't know.'

'I mean, was it reported, or was she buried, or – what?'

'I really don't know. My father dealt with it.'

'Of course, your father was still around. I forgot.' I thought about him. 'Do you think he knew?'

'That Cass was murdered? I've always assumed so, yes.'

'And do you think he knew who it was? Who did it?'

'Again, I've assumed so. I've always assumed he thought it was me. Mother would've told him it was me, I'm sure.' He thought about it, at once less sure. 'I suppose it's possible he didn't know. She might have lied to him to protect me, or . . .'

'Or to protect herself? She might have told him it was an accident?'

'It's possible, I suppose.'

'Although he might not have believed her, of course. He might have been convinced it was she who'd killed his little girl. It would be as good a reason as any to leave your wife, wouldn't it? And he did leave her, didn't he? Pretty soon afterwards.'

'Two weeks later, yes.'

He fell silent. Thoughtful.

'Did you never see him again at all?'

'No, not until . . .'

He didn't finish the sentence. In fact he plainly regretted having started it. He had let something slip unintentionally. He coloured a little.

'Until when, Howard?'

'Until never. I never saw him again. At all.'

He smiled nervously. He could see that I didn't believe him.

'But I did hear from him. That was all I meant. He wrote when Katherine died. To say how sorry he was. It was rather a surprise, since I'd more or less given him up for dead.'

'Perhaps you should correspond with him. See what he can remember. He might finally be able to put your mind at rest.'

'Wouldn't that be a glorious thing?' he said, like a hunted man for whom the word 'rest' implies an impossible, longed-for dream.

'He might know something really crucial,' I said.

'Yes. I haven't had time, unfortunately, since Katherine died, to ask him anything . . .'

We stood staring out of the window like two goldfish, side by side. His proximity thrilled me unfailingly from that day henceforward. That falling-in-love day. I thought about the probable quantities of women in his life. I tried to imagine one or two. Why did he never mention them?

'That woman you loved,' I ventured bravely, out of the blue, 'who was she?'

'Which woman?'

'The one you lost.'

'I've lost many women, Mo.'

Was I merely one in an endless line, I wondered.

'The one you spoke about before, with the diaries – the one who killed herself.'

'Oh. Lizzie. Yes. Lizzie,' he said reflectively.

'Lizzie?'

'Yes, she was the first.'

'The first – woman? Or the first one to kill herself?'

'The first one to run!' He was making light of it, but it didn't seem especially light.

'You said that reading her diaries brought something up for you, some question came up . . .'

'Did I?'

His eyes were like the lens of a microscope now, focusing on the centre of my soul. He seemed to be assessing whether I was worthy of a further confidence.

'Lizzie and I were – engaged. My first true love.'

'How old were you?'

'Thirty-eight . . .'

Thirty-eight seemed too old for a man's first love, but I said nothing.

'The question that came up in Lizzie's diary – well, it's the same question. It's the question I have about Cass –'

'Murder?'

'Attempted, in this instance. But murder, yes.'

Don't panic, I told myself. Hear him out.

'According to her diaries,' he continued, 'and I had no knowledge of this until I read them – but apparently, the very night after we'd announced our engagement, while she was staying in one of the guest bedrooms here, someone tried to suffocate her.'

'Jesus. Who?'

'In the middle of the night. Pitch dark. She had no idea who it was. She couldn't see anything. She even lost consciousness. Presumably whoever it was thought they'd killed her. The following morning she left, unsurprisingly. She never came back.'

'God,' was all I dared say, in case he was about to confess.

'There were only two people in the house. My mother and myself.' He paused, letting the silence speak for itself. 'It's the same problem, isn't it? It has to have been one of us.'

'Was it?'

'Lizzie assumed it was me. My mother had already frightened her enough with tales of Cassandra's murder. Why wouldn't she suspect me?' He looked at me as if hoping for a reason why not, but sadly none suggested itself. 'She killed herself all these years later because she "finally couldn't face the evil in the world". And who can blame her?'

The old fear crept back. However much I wanted to trust him, I couldn't. I couldn't believe in his innocence until he believed in it himself. How can you trust someone who tells you they can't trust themselves? All you can do is offer your company.

I searched his face.

'You think it was me, too,' he said.

'I don't know, Howard. I don't know what to think.'

'I need proof. That's what I need.'

'How are you getting along?' came a piping, cheerful voice behind us. The old boy was beaming from ear to ear. How much had he heard, standing in the doorway unobserved?

'I do hope I didn't frighten you,' he said.

'Not at all,' said Howard, disguising his agitation poorly.

'Only I wondered if you'd care for some tea?'

'Thank you. Why not?'

'I shall be in the kitchen, then,' he said, and he left us to follow him.

We stood in silence for a while, smiling at each other like old friends with old jokes to share. But the seriousness soon returned.

'I only read Lizzie's diaries after my mother's death,' Howard explained, 'a month ago,' as if the timing was an important factor to grasp.

'How come?'

'Well, I had very little interest in her by the time she died. Ten years is a long time. And I'd cut her out entirely from my thoughts when she left. I was very hurt . . .' Pause. 'Kittie was a great comfort to me, though, during that time. I was soon back to normal.' Whatever 'normal' was, I thought.

The kitchen was damp and grubby, its paint an ageing custard yellow. An old Aga of the same colour had been chipped and dented over the years, but spread a general warmth throughout the room. I wondered if it was the same kitchen Howard had known as a child. He looked about him with a certain nostalgia. And a certain hostility, too.

The old boy seemed to be studying us out of the corner of his eye. Some hidden agenda that I couldn't begin to guess at was absorbing him.

'Lovely cup of tea,' I said.

'Indian,' he replied. 'Always the best.'

Howard looked up at him abruptly.

'Indian tea!' said the old boy again, playfully shouting at him.

'What about it?' asked Howard coldly, but no explanation was offered.

'I went to India once,' I said. 'I loved it. I remember my journey up to Darjeeling most particularly, on a tiny two-carriager –'

'Isn't that a terrific little trip?' said the old boy enthusiastically.

Howard looked up from his tea again in disbelief.

'Have you been to India?' he asked.

'No, no, not at all,' said the old boy adamantly, 'I've only read about it.'

'Then you should be careful, sir. You make yourself sound like a man of the world!'

He was half joking and half putting the old boy down. I didn't like it.

I looked out of the window at the garden. It looked sinister in the half-light of the dusk, an inextricable knot of roses and thorns. The evening was coming in fast. It was still raining hard, the sky dark and gloomy and promising more of the same.

'I ought to get back to London soon,' I said.

'And so you shall, so you shall . . .'

I had expressed my wish to Howard but the old man had answered me. Howard was deep in thought.

I wondered what I was doing in this remote place with these two strange men. I could feel the malevolent atmosphere contaminate me like a disease. Like a plague? Contracted through thin air?

'Howard? Shouldn't we be getting back?'

'Back?'

'To London.'

'If you like.'

He didn't seem keen.

'If you want to stay, I can easily get a train. Just drop me at the station. Salisbury's not far, is it?'

'No, we'll go.'

Pause.

'You could always stay over. Rough night for a drive,' suggested the old boy.

Howard looked at me for some hint of willingness. I felt none. In fact I positively dreaded the thought of a whole night there.

'That's very kind, but I have a husband to get back to. He must be wondering where I am.'

This felt like a lie, so remote were Bill and I from each other now. But as an excuse to escape the toxicity, it served me well.

'A husband! Well, well!' he exclaimed. 'The other one has a husband, too, as I remember it! So many husbands and wives.'

'Can we wash up for you before we go?' Howard cut in.

'What other one?' I asked.

Howard began to stack up the plates and cups.

'The other woman,' said the old boy.

'Who?' I was asking Howard now.

'I don't know what he's talking about.'

'What other woman?' I asked the old man.

Just as he was about to answer me, Howard dropped the

pile of crockery on the cold stone floor. When the noise of it stopped echoing in my ears, I looked at Howard's trembling face.

'I'm so sorry,' he said, seeming as baffled as I was by his action. He knelt down to retrieve the scattered pieces of china. 'I'm terribly sorry, sir. I shall replace these, of course.'

Had it been deliberate, then?

I was burning with curiosity about this other woman, but with great self-restraint I let things be.

'D'you want a hand?' I offered.

'It's quite all right, thank you. The least I can do is clear it up myself.'

After a short silence, I found myself spilling over with laughter – the kind of laughter I used to restrain as a schoolgirl, nervous and totally inappropriate, making it doubly compelling. The old man also began to laugh, for reasons of his own, emitting such wild, shrill noises that even Howard was amused. By the end of the evening we were all laughing uncontrollably. But at quite different things, I felt sure.

10

I woke early. It was still so dark that I could barely see where I was. What little I could disntinguish was only vaguely familiar to me. How had I got here? Had I been drugged? Reviewing the previous day's excursions, I surmised that it had to be one of two places: Chiswick or Wiltshire. With North.

Neither possibility seemed wholesome at that early hour. I wondered why. I had always found the first hour of the day to be the most illuminating, the time at which I could hear most clearly the good sense of my unconscious mind. The common sense, deep in all of us. Like a conscience, or a god. That morning the sense was especially distinct. I had taken a wrong turning. I had lost my way.

The filled-in pond like a home-made grave haunted me. I dreaded the morning light, dreaded finding myself in Katherine's room, seeing the room again, the pond again, the tangled garden below. But although I missed my regular days, safe as a timetable, I felt no immediate urge to return to them. How could I forgo this adventure in my life for mere safety's sake? I was enthralled. I can think of no better word. Afraid, but enthralled.

This intelligence Howard wanted from me, this head, not heart, of me: why was it so crucial to him? Or did he really mean detachment? Objectivity? He certainly wasn't encouraging any emotion in me. Not willingly, at least. My feelings were troublesome enough as it was. He was asking for analysis, almost. But then, why come to me? I believed in empathy, above all. Objective thought was for people who could no longer see the wood for the trees. Couldn't Howard? Was that it? Was he too much in the thick of this to find his own way through? How dense a wood was it, then?

I imagined a mass of enmeshed branches strangling each other, strangling anything in their midst, suffocating all life. I thought again of the garden, the wild roses and thorns, menacing as snakes in the half-light. I could see Howard in there, gasping for breath. The image was surely a warning of sorts.

Would I have to join him there?

I had the sense of being asked to visit hell itself, with no guarantee that I would ever return.

I did go back to sleep. The sedative of sleep. I dreamt of the cold again and woke to find myself naked beneath a single sheet in a room now light enough for me to recognize. Katherine's room. Panic set in. I had lain awake, I recalled, for much of the night, anticipating suffocation at the very least. Now I half-expected to find Katherine standing over me with a knife, grinning like a fiend, a fearful menace in her eyes. I breathed deep and long, until the rhythm calmed me. What was I so afraid of in her? What dread beast threatened my life? Certainly she was the particular form that my terror took, but did something far worse lie beneath the mere symbol of her?

Before I had climbed out of bed, let alone considered the full implications of this question, there was a gentle knock on the door.

'Who is it?'

'Mo?'

Howard's voice, like a timid boy's.

'I'm not up yet.'

'Can I come in?'

'Hold on, I'll just . . .' I reached for my T-shirt in amongst my discarded clothes and slipped it over my head. 'OK, come in,' I said.

He opened and closed the door without a sound, seeming to breathe more easily as soon as this was done.

'What's the matter?'

'Nothing. Are you all right?'

'Why? Shouldn't I be?'

'Did you sleep even half-decently?'

'Not bad,' I said, lying. 'You?'

'I found it quite impossible to – er – to sleep, myself.'

He was propping his exhausted body up against the door like a stringless manikin.

'It must be hard for you, coming here.'

He was staring at me very intently, not really listening to me. He was deeply preoccupied.

'What is it?' I asked, uncomfortably. 'Why are you staring at me like that?'

'I was just . . .' But he changed the subject abruptly. 'Look, do you want to go back up to London today or can you spend a little more time with me?'

'Howard, I'm a married woman. I have a life of my own.'

I was using Bill like a shield.

'I know that,' he said irritably.

'How do I explain this excursion to my husband?' As if he would care . . .

'He doesn't own you.'

'Neither do you.'

But his face said, yes I do – I own the very heart of you.

'I want to be back by this evening,' I said, matter-of-factly. 'OK?'

He nodded and smiled like a child.

'I want to dig up the pond,' he said, equally matter-of-fact. I shuddered at the thought.

'Why?'

'To see if there are any clues. I want proof,' he said. 'I must find proof.' He paused. 'Help me. You must help me, Mo.'

It was an order, really, lightly disguised as a plea. I flattered myself that I had some choice in the matter, but if I'd chosen to walk away then, I would have found out the truth.

11

The wind was biting cold, eating into my flesh like a parasite. We were crouching over the once-upon-a-time pond, six foot across, and digging away at the compacted soil with hopelessly heavy old spades.

It's going to be a visit to hell and back just digging this bloody thing, I muttered to myself.

'Eh?'

Howard had his back to me, digging the end that faced south. My direction was north, so that when the sun occasionally burst through I could enjoy the warmth of it on my back. One of few comforts that day. Facing north also meant that I could study the back of the house and observe how frequently the little old man's white head of hair appeared at one window or another. By midday I had counted eighteen occasions, and I must have missed a few.

After approximately four hours of unrewarding, unremitting work, I hit gold. The spadeful of dark wet earth glinted at me like a lighthouse at night. My impulse was to tell Howard immediately, before I had even seen what it was, but a deeper, more suspicious impulse suggested that I keep it to myself, just for the time being. The impulse of fear. I fingered the sodden soil like a detective, cautious and respectful of perhaps the only clue – vital evidence that could clear or condemn a soul. It offered up a small gold locket, about the size of a coin. Exquisitely engraved.

I stopped breathing. I was a thief now, hot and furtive, fearful of being caught. I stuffed the treasure into my pocket, committing myself to a more thorough examination at some later, lonelier hour.

'Irksome task, this . . .' Howard shouted across to me in the wind.

He seemed to be enjoying the simple physical objective of the day, a robust and invigorating contrast to his more cerebral preoccupations, whatever those were.

'Telling me!' I called back jovially.

The paradox of our high spirits in the face of this morbid mission did not escape me. Perhaps it was a natural reaction in the face of such a grim pursuit, but I still felt ashamed. And this shame extended to my guilty secret now, burning in my pocket like a hot coal. Howard's insistence upon truth as the ultimate morality had me sinning already. Betraying him.

Hours later the old man brought up a thermos flask of weak Darjeeling tea and inedible sandwiches, and admitted to the name of Rolf. Howard raised an eyebrow in disbelief and smiled discreetly at me.

'What's that short for, then . . . Roland the Wolf?' And he barked at the old man like a dog. 'Rolf! Rolf!'

'Rolf' seemed to find this enormously funny.

'Oh, I see! Yes, indeed! Very witty indeed!' He could hardly breathe for chuckling. 'Rolf! Rolf! Rolf! Rolf!' He barked somewhat ferociously at both of us before adding very flatly: 'It's not short for anything at all, in fact.'

There was something incongruent about him. Something hidden. For a start, I felt quite sure that his real name was not Rolf. Then there was his moodiness which, unlike Howard's, seemed implausibly controllable. It was not as if there was a dark unsettled area of his soul that suddenly pushed through into the light, but a cool, considered change of direction, seemingly designed to put one off the scent. A versatile chameleon disguised as an eccentric old man. Then there was the fact that he was there at all. What would an old man want with a remote country house that size?

'Is this your part of the world, Rolf?' I asked.

'I've lived here long enough!' he said cheerfully, his humour masking his unwillingness to say more.

'How long is long enough?' I persevered, equally cheerfully.

'I've quite lost count of the years, my dear.' He finished the sentence as if with a full stop. In fact he was just about to launch into a new chapter heading when I asked:

'Many years, then?'

'Many years. Off and on.' Another full stop.

'Off and on' intrigued me. Somehow I couldn't imagine this man to be 'off and on' about anything. Was I making assumptions again? I sensed that he was a man who could not tell lies easily and who therefore had to be rather vague about the truths he wished to conceal. After all, the lie of his own name had escaped neither Howard nor myself. It was blatant. I thought I could probably draw the truth out of him with a little time and my characteristic stubbornness, but I was optimistic, as it turned out.

'It's getting dark already,' said Howard, looking up at the heavy sky accusingly. 'God, I hate this wretched time of year.'

'Shall we call it a day?' I suggested, easy either way, but aware of the long motorway journey ahead.

He ran his eyes over me as if they were his hands, caressing my cold limbs. I could feel myself light up like a dry bonfire, suddenly ablaze.

'You want to get back, don't you?' he asked.

I want to lie beside you on white sand . . .

'I really should,' I said.

'Want to, or should?'

'Both. Does it matter? The outcome is the same.'

Howard clearly didn't suspect the old man as I did. He talked in front of 'Rolf' as if he were senile or deaf or both.

'It matters to me.'

'Well . . .' I said blandly, not wanting to be drawn. I looked down at the dry pond, away from him.

I heard him sigh. A sad sigh. I didn't dare look up until I had seen his feet tread a fair distance to the house.

I cannot be all things to all men, I told myself. The fever will pass.

'She loved him, that woman.'

The old man was standing very close to me, his voice steady and sane as it had not yet been.

'Who?'

He didn't answer.

'His mother, you mean?'

'Well, I wouldn't know about that . . .'

'Wouldn't you?' I asked.

He smiled mildly.

'Who then?' I demanded. The other woman, of course, I answered myself. 'Who was she, this other woman?'

'Ah, I could describe her face to you, but her name . . . I never remember names.'

'Not even your own, huh?'

He gave me a long, honest stare. It said: Be very careful. The ground upon which you stand is dangerous. I tell you for your own good.

'I wouldn't like to be in her shoes now,' was what he actually voiced.

'Why not?'

But he looked away towards the house, as if to be sure that Howard was nowhere nearby.

'She was just like you,' he said. 'Only . . . a sure woman. Sure of herself.'

'How much like me?'

'She said she had a twin,' he replied simply. Confirmation of my worst fears.

'Why are you telling me this?'

'For your own good.'

He shuffled away then, leaving me on the uncertain ground of the buried pond.

Kate? What was her game?

I followed him inside, the soft darkness of dusk eerie as the previous evening, uncertain shadows dancing before me. I longed for some concrete truth, some absolute in all this possibility. Glimpses of certainty evaporated like mist in the half-light of impending night.

The same cold, fluorescent tube welcomed me in the kitchen. The old man was stirring some odious concoction from a tin in a heavy saucepan over the Aga.

'Is that your tea?'

'It's Kitty's tea.'

'Glad to hear it. Where's Howard?'

'Upstairs?'

I took off the wellington boots that we'd brought down from Chiswick after the walk in Richmond Park, and made my way upstairs in the almost-dark.

'Howard?'

I knocked on several doors before finding his.

'Hello?' came his disembodied voice.

'Can I come in?'

He didn't answer.

I found him lying on his bed staring blankly up at the ceiling.

'Sorry to intrude.'

'What is it?'

'I was just wondering when you were thinking of heading off.'

'Heading off what?'

'I mean, heading for London. Going.'

He exhaled again, the same sad sigh.

'Whenever you like.'

'There's no need to make me feel so bad, is there?'

'Oh, for heaven's sake!' he exclaimed wearily. 'Here we go again . . .'

'Sorry?'

'Good. Bad. Right. Wrong. Black. White. What's the matter with you? Can't you see how intolerably grey everything is?'

'No, I can't,' I said firmly.

'No, you can't, can you? I almost envy you your simple view of things.'

'There's no need to pass a value judgement on my view of things.'

'I expect you think you're closer to God, don't you, with all that simplicity?'

'No.'

'Of course you do. Just the way you say "no" like that, so smug and sure of yourself.'

Sure of yourself. The words rang in my ears.

I didn't know what was happening. From those caressing eyes to this inability even to look at me. Had he witnessed my exchange with the old man? Was I no longer to be trusted?

I remembered the locket in my pocket and felt for it anxiously. Still there. I was not to be trusted, no.

'I think I'll just call a cab, Howard. Make my own way back.'

I closed the door behind me. He didn't look at me once.

The cab took two hours to arrive. I used the time fruitfully, prowling through the house more stealthily than either Kitty the cat or Kittie the ghost, unnoticed by anyone.

The most surprising and perplexing of my discoveries was the abundant evidence of the latter's presence. Her belongings were everywhere. It seemed as if no one had collected them after her death, as if the place waited for her as it always had done in brief absences. Her name was in every book, her initials on everything from napkin rings to cutlery to hairbrushes, her dried flowers spilt out of old albums, what I assumed were her clothes still hung in the wardrobes, and a virtual tower of mail awaited her on the hall table.

Nothing had been touched. A thick coating of dust covered the furniture, disrupted only by an occasional item of Rolf's, strewn about the place – a book or a pipe or an out-of-date newspaper. In the main the possessions were hers, as was the house. Her return seemed imminent. It waited for her animation like a stage-set ready for a play. Suspended in time, impervious to death, this house expected her.

I would find out. I would find out everything.

Despite my investigative boldness in the house, I did not dare to draw from my pocket the buried treasure I had found. I longed to open it up, for I was sure there was some vital clue inside, but I would do so only behind a locked door in my own home.

Howard did not reappear from his room, and I chose not to bid him goodbye, but I saw the curtain twitch as I climbed into the back seat of the taxi.

12

When I got home Bill was in the living-room listening to Wagner and reading psychology books. I tiptoed upstairs unnoticed and locked myself in the bathroom. I was nervous of what I might find in the locket. I dreaded most some evidence of the dead child herself. Some lock of hair, or a fingernail.

Why a fingernail? The thought was morbid and very unlikely but almost paralysed my willingness to look inside.

I turned on the hot tap and held the treasured clue beneath its flow, careful not to let any water leak into the locket itself. Once free of the mud, I could see that the chain had been broken, as if ripped or pulled from the owner's neck. It was a longish chain, without doubt an adult's. No small drowned child had once worn a chain this long. The locket must have belonged to Katherine, and been wrenched from her in a struggle by the pond. With her husband? Or with Howard? Or with little Cassie herself? This was evidence of sorts, wasn't it?

My own fingernails were short and struggled in vain to release the catch. Frustration eclipsed any hesitation I had felt. My impatience mounted into an intense battle with this small delicate thing. I applied a nail file, tweezers, nail scissors and finally a razor-blade without success. I found myself about to stamp on it like a petulant child. Intelligence, Mo, I told myself. Head, not heart . . .

I studied the locket right up close. It was as tight as a fresh mussel, stubborn, unyielding, like a safe casement hiding its secret from me. Then suddenly, without any interference from me, it sprang open and her face was staring at mine, a mirror of mine, her eyes as large and seeing as the sun.

My heart hit at my ribs like a frantic animal trapped in a sudden cage. She seemed in the room with me for that instant. It shocked me as an accident would, leaving me dazed and confused, surprised by my continuing breath. The effect was so overwhelming, it was as if I had met a ghost, as if I had been visited by another's will, a presence, a force of some kind.

I sat on the side of the bath, breathing deeply. It was a while before I dared to look at the locket again. When I did, I noticed a second photograph, on the other side. A young man, whose face was strangely familiar, although I couldn't think when or where I had seen it. A face from a Russian play or film, like Chekhov's face. There was the same sadness about his eyes that moved me. They seemed almost to be pleading with me. I didn't feel any visitation when I looked at him, but when I shifted my focus back to Katherine's photograph, I felt her there again, less suddenly and more certainly.

She was undeniably beautiful. Her fine, delicate features framed her exquisite eyes like precious metal around two radiant jewels.

How could any man withstand her? Even her own son must have been in love with her. And how could any woman be both as beautiful as she was and good? Decent? Honourable? Who wouldn't use such a gift as that for their own ends, even unconsciously? Could she know any other way?

I tried to temper my innate hostility, my envy of her, with some feeling of sisterhood, some generosity. It was a struggle. Envy came easily to me after so many years of Kate. I could always see qualities in other people that I failed to see in myself, and somehow it would always seem as though they had got my share.

I saw that in the photograph Katherine was actually wearing the locket, and had one hand stretched out towards it as if superstitiously checking its presence. I could see a frail vulnerability in that hand. She was, of course, gazing intently not at me but at this young man, who must have been her husband. I thought of what Howard had told me about their relationship, and I felt a deep empathy at last. A deep knowledge of her.

This feeling calmed me. I felt able to put the locket away, as though I had heard what she had come to say. I thought it was safest in my own jewellery box for the time being.

I went downstairs to greet Bill but he was fast asleep, snoring lightly. I sat down beside him, needing the warmth of him, the old familiar smell of his life. I felt like a thief again, stealing parts of him without his consent. I drowsed in the rhythm of his breath until I was also asleep.

The curtains had been left open and the early morning sun poured through them in a flood of gold. Particular words ran through my semi-consciousness like the headings of important paragraphs. Home. Warmth. Love. Marriage. Family. Bill. And finally Husband, tagged on the end.

We seemed so close again, lying against each other in the sun. Marriage should be for ever this. Soft bliss. The ordinary warmth of old intimacy, won with the effortful years. But we had lost it for ever in a careless day or two.

As soon as consciousness invaded us, however, the air turned cold. Bill pulled away from me and sat up suddenly, cricking his neck and back. He had an alarming ability to realign his spine without a chiropractor so that it cracked and crunched murderously, threatening to do irrevocable harm.

'Is it all right?'

'Yup,' came the monosyllabic reply.

We were silent, our bodies awkwardly close, with an emotional distance of miles. A vast acreage.

'How's your piece coming along?' I asked, politely, almost, as if of a stranger.

'OK.'

I reckoned that two syllables were better than one and that three might be on their way. I glanced over the titles spread across the floor.

'Heavy reading, by the looks of it.'

'Yup.'

I was wrong about the syllables.

We both stared out at the garden, frozen in the clean, clear sun.

'Is it interesting? Paedophilia?'

'Very.'

'Disturbing, I guess, researching it?'

He nodded.

'I think it's much more common than people realize,' he said.

A whole sentence encouraged me further.

'The actual practice of it, you mean, or just the desire?'

'Both.' He climbed over me and stood up. 'Want some tea?'

'Please.'

Please don't turn away, old friend. Allow me my adventure. Please?

He went next door. I glanced again at his books on deviant sexual behaviour. Why was he allowed to delve deep beneath the safe surface of things if I wasn't? Why condemn my small curiosity?

I thumbed through one of these books, intrigued despite myself. *Young Sexuality*, it was called. There were other, less appealing titles that I chose to ignore.

Bill returned with two large mugs of tea and a packet of biscuits.

'I didn't get to Sainsbury's, I'm afraid.'

He struggled with the impenetrably tight plastic wrapping. I gulped the hot strong tea. I held the book oafishly in one hand, like an unwelcome visitor in my own sweet home, wanting to reach into our lost marriage for a handful of ease.

He finally freed the biscuits and offered me one.

'Thanks.'

We ate them quietly, glancing at each other and glancing away.

A silence full of unsaid things.

'Have you been with . . . ?' he asked tentatively.

'Yes, I have,' I said plainly. Cleanly. Unsuggestively.

He picked up a book. One might call this a displacement activity, but it seemed well-placed to me. It seemed like sorrow.

'People always talk about children as if they're a different breed, like dogs or something,' he said irrelevantly. He was waving the book about as if referring to it, but he was distracting me with it, in fact, while his eyes searched me for tell-tale signs of betrayal.

'A different breed?' I said, letting him search, letting things be what they were.

'As if they only become human when their sexuality begins . . .'

'But it begins at birth.'

'Exactly!' he said. 'But everyone pretends it begins at puberty. Why? It obviously doesn't, does it? Doctors-and-nurses starts at about age three.'

He fell silent again, looking at me as if I was someone he didn't know very well.

'I don't think that's true, actually,' I said. 'Paedophiles often make out that the kids lead them on, don't they? As if they're very sexual.'

'That's what I'm saying, Mo. They act surprised that the kids lead them on. Why? Kids are openly sexual little beings. They want to explore sex. Why expect them to be paragons of virtue, innocent of sexual desire? That's when the harm is done.'

'Maybe,' I said.

'The harm is done when adults pretend their kids aren't sexual. They seduce them in all sorts of subtle ways, and then when the kids reach puberty and they can perform sexually, the shit hits the fan.'

I wondered why this was all so important to him.

'It's a difficult line,' I said.

'What is?'

'Sex and kids.'

'Is it?' he said, as if it shouldn't be a difficult line.

'I can sort of understand how it happens, can't you?'

'Can you?'

He was shocked, as if my empathy meant that I condoned it in some way, or even that I was capable of such abuse myself.

'I can see how the line gets crossed, how it becomes hazy, ill-defined. A lonely adult, with the undivided attention of an adoring child of the opposite sex who wants to touch and be touched. I can sort of understand. I mean I find it very hard to understand how an adult can do actual sex with a kid. But subtle seduction, or "molestation", as I suppose it would be called, I can see how that happens.'

He looked disgusted by me.

'Thank God we lost our child in that case.'

I felt as if I'd been knifed.

'I'm not saying I would have molested him, Bill! I'm saying I'm conscious of that capacity in human beings under certain circumstances.'

'And you a therapist! A The Rapist.'

'God, you're so repressed!'

We were heading for another full-blown, hurtful, spiteful row.

'I'm so repressed, am I? So repressed I believe in saving our marriage, is that what you mean? Whereas all your fucking stupid therapy has taught you is how to screw more than one man and still sleep peacefully at night! After everything you've said to me. After everything you've accused me of, you rip our marriage to bits!'

He was shouting now. I was probably shouting myself.

'What fucking marriage? Since when were you trying to save our marriage, Bill? Because I didn't notice. And I don't want it saved any more.'

'Fine.' He took this in. 'Thanks for telling me.'

'There's nothing left to save.'

'I disagree. But you're obviously so obsessed with Howard Nor –'

'How come it's all right for you to go off for days on end, week in, week out, but it's not all right for me? It's not OK for me to want to work –'

'I go away to research a subject. A subject, Mo. You're interested in one person who wants to fuck you stupid. OK. Fair enough.'

'I'm not just interested in him, although I'll admit he's a lot more interesting than anything else that's happened in the last ten years –'

'Are you in love with him?'

'What I'm interested in,' I said, unwilling to answer that, 'is the whole family, the whole set-up, the "story", as you would say. I'm after the story.'

'I'll tell you a story, honey. Just ask, you know? It's my department, stories . . .'

'Why is it your bloody department?'

'Shall I tell you one now?'

'Bill, I'm trying to explain things to you – are you listening or not?'

'Come to think of it, you probably know it already.'

'Know what?' I shouted impatiently.

'It was probably the first thing he confessed to you.'

'Confessed to me?'

The word sent a shudder through me.

'In your intimate little sessions together.'

'Confessed?' I asked again, my voice deserting me, leaving only a whisper. Bill had that smug look of triumph on his face, familiar in cruel children.

'What, Bill?' And, when he didn't answer, 'What's he done?'

'Or maybe you're that fucking nuts that you can hear a confession like that and not turn him in. No, worse than that, set him on a pedestal, set him apart, the Man Who Dared . . .'

I glared at him in horror, knowing that he could mean only one thing. The thing I dreaded the most. He could only mean murder. Little Cassie's drowned body was Howard's doing after all. Bill had somehow found out, with his journalistic prowess, what I was still only guessing at.

'How do you know?'

'How do I know what?'

'Come on, Bill. Don't play games. How do you know?'

'No, wait. What do you know, Mo?'

He wanted the words, the actual words, spoken in my voice.

'I know about a murder. OK?'

'You *know*? You do know?'

'Well . . .'

'He actually told you?'

I was being tricked into breaking any confidentiality that remained between Howard and myself.

'I can't say any more.'

'We're talking about murder, Mo.'

'It's unethical.'

'Murder? You're telling me!'

'I mean I can't break confidentiality.'

'How convenient.'

After a short, shared silence, he added:

'I understand from Kate that confidentiality breaks down when a client is a danger either to himself or to anyone else.'

'So it was Kate who told you, was it?'

'Never reveal your sources. Rule Number One.'

'Not even when they're a danger to themselves or anyone else?'

He didn't answer me.

'Pretty tight with Kate these days, aren't you?'

He didn't answer. He simply stared at me, a look of tired frustration on his face. Then he said in a flat, honest voice:

'There's such a stupid, blind arrogance about you these days, Mo.'

The words hurt, if only because he didn't intend them to. He was just stating a fact. He added:

'You think you're invincible. You think bad things won't ever happen to you. But you're wrong. Be told, Mo. You're wrong.'

'He was only a boy,' I said, as if this was an acceptable excuse. 'He lacked awareness.'

'What are you talking about?'

I was trying to make Howard's crime bearable to myself. Forgivable, even.

'He was only a little boy.'

'He's a fully grown man, Mo!'

'Now he is, obviously. When he did it, I mean.'

'He "did it" about a month ago!'

'What!'

My blood ran cold. We were suddenly talking about something quite different, about which I knew nothing and for which I was not prepared.

'What are you talking about now?'

'Darling, don't you know?'

'What?'

'He was a chief suspect. Or still is. He had no alibi. But because there weren't any witnesses, and there wasn't enough circumstantial evidence, they couldn't detain him. But they still suspect him.'

'Of what?'

'His mother's murder. Howard North's mother was murdered about a month ago. Surely you've just said you know that, Mo?'

'No. I didn't know that.'

'But you've just said he confessed.'

'No, I didn't. I was talking about something else.'

'You mean he killed someone else?'

'No, I don't mean that. Stop confusing me.'

'If you're protecting him, Mo . . .'

'*I'm not protecting him!*' I suddenly bellowed, stunning us both into silence. 'His little sister was drowned when he was a boy. He's haunted by it. Nobody really knows how it happened.'

'I'll hazard a guess!' He was almost laughing, as though the obviousness was too pronounced for any but the most obtuse to miss. 'It's that murder which is weighing so heavily against him now. He's just been released for the second time. Second arrest. Still no evidence. Just questioning.'

I could feel the tears, hot and uncontrollable, coursing down my cheeks. His voice was kind at once, but no comfort to me. Too late now.

'Come on, baby, sit down. It's all right, sit down.'

He steered me back to the sofa and sat me down, cradling me like a baby in his arms, while I wept.

'He didn't do it,' I said.

'It's all right . . . sshhh . . .'

'I'll prove he didn't.'

'That's right . . .' he hummed, humouring me.

'Poor Howard.'

'All right baby . . .' he stroked my hair. 'All right now.'

'I'm fine,' I said.

'Do you want something to eat?'

'Not really.'

'I could go to Sainsbury's – get something nice?'

'Could do.'

He thought I was almost his, almost back again in one piece.

When he was gone I sobbed. My private grief, the grief I couldn't show Bill, betrayed the depth of my involvement with North. It was the same uncontrollable grief that hit me when my parents died. I was up to my neck. Treading water. Feeling only his tides, his particular ebbs and flows.

Bill came back with lobster, cheeses, rye bread and Chardonnay. We ate with the silver cutlery and lit a candle which danced in the morning sun. He said that we should talk of the murders again, the seriousness of them, but that today should be a day of peace.

We would have made tender love in our big bed, if there had been a marriage left to save. But there wasn't. We both knew that.

13

I was sick for days after that meal, or possibly weeks. I blamed the sickness on the lobster, but it was more likely the Plague. In truth, my stomach was such a knot of fear that it would have heaved at anything. I felt as if my body was protesting, as if it was rejecting what I clung to in my mind, or heart, or soul – whichever domain it was that Howard now dominated. I couldn't bear to let him go.

The thought that Howard had murdered his own mother was too repulsive to allow. I would not allow it. I denied it with all my power. And yet curiously, when I almost allowed it, the murder of Cassie seemed as nothing by comparison. This disturbed me, this relativism of violent crime, as though once a line was irreversibly crossed, other lines could be sketched in along the way to comfort the conscience: harms not yet done. So if he had killed his sister, well, at least he hadn't killed his mother. Yet.

I slept fitfully during my illness. At moments of relative calm I would suddenly be seized by a horror so deep that death seemed the only likely relief. I would wonder at such times how anyone who had survived a war could ever find life bearable again. Let alone meaningful. Then I would sleep a little. The drug of unconsciousness. These short bursts of rest would lull me into a false sense of security from which I would wake with a sudden sense of peace. I would feel the shape of hope again.

But then I would start thinking. Howard's words, 'right' and 'wrong' and 'truth', would float through my mind, and I would argue things out in my head. Was he trying to justify a multitude of terrible, hidden crimes with this new morality of his? Was I so lost in the complexities and contradictions of his baffling brain that I couldn't trust my common sense any more? Was I hiding from the dark truth?

If he has committed either murder, I told myself, he has crossed that line. And if he's crossed that line . . . then what? I'll find out the truth. If he is a murderer, I'll turn him in.

I presented myself to myself as something of a saviour, a truth-seeker, on the surface of things. I had a cause, and it gave me a reason to march out of my empty life once more. I had to prove his innocence. I had to keep the truth sweet.

When I recovered physically, I was in a state of such mental delusion that I couldn't even see the danger I was in. I felt that I was – and indeed I could appear to be – as lucid as light itself. But real light illuminates real things, and I had lost my sense of reality by then.

While Bill was struggling to meet his deadline for whichever Saturday national newspaper it was, I packed a few necessities into a small suitcase and left.

He didn't hear the door shut, the car start. He was listening to an interview he had taped, with the volume turned up very loud to hear the voice above the background noise. It was a woman's voice, explaining why she had kept her son in her own bed at night until he was almost grown up.

I stood a short while in the hall, listening.

Her husband had died, she said, when her son was four. They both cried so loud in their separate beds, it seemed a crime not to comfort each other by cuddling up together instead of sleeping apart. And then they just sort of got into the habit of it.

I was tempted to stay long enough to hear what became of them, especially the pubescent son, but my prurient interest shamed me.

I drove past Howard's house in search of some evidence that he had returned from the West Country. He had. The Mercedes was lolling in the drive.

I pulled up by the kerb and crunched a path through the gravel to the front door, where I knocked on the big brass door-knocker. No one answered. I waited for some minutes because I thought I saw a shape or a shadow move across the window of the front room, but if I did, whoever it was didn't want to know me.

Was it Howard?

I felt that I had failed him in some way. Could he sense that I had broken his confidences and even hidden vital clues from him, and that now I suspected him myself? Could he see me for the traitor I was? I felt sure that he could. I sensed that he could see me now, see through me, waiting on his doorstep like a dog. He could see my deceit, my suspicion, my treachery, clear as daylight, and he was shutting me out of his life.

This thought sharpened my determination to force my way back in. I had to prove myself, my worthiness, my trustworthiness to him.

I waited in my car, flicking through a book of Neville Hoare's about personal responsibility. Just to pass the time. It didn't tell me anything I didn't already know.

My car was parked on the same side of the road as Howard's house, hidden from view by the wall that adjoined the gates to his drive. He would have to walk or drive out in front of my windscreen if he was there at all. I would see anyone who came or went from the house.

I was a truth-seeker, I flattered myself, with right on my side. A private investigator, there to see justice done. I enjoyed the self-importance of this fantasy. It glorified my ordinary, unfulfilled ineffectiveness.

I read the end of the book, looking for conclusions, hoping for some affirmation of my actions as valid and worthy. I found instead an essay on vanity. Hoare called it the major motivating force behind most 'good deeds'. I felt irritated and depressed by a world-view that would once have seemed to me honest and sane.

I put the book back in my suitcase and stared out at the road ahead. I must have sat there for at least an hour before anything happened. And then Kate swept past the front of my car and she was out of sight, speeding away in her BMW.

14

On the motorway I tried to remember everything Howard had ever said to me, but nothing formed even half a sentence. My head was a cacophony of words and voices, none of which made any sense.

The road was wet and the rain still heavy. My wiper blade needed changing months ago, in the rain-free summer months, and I regretted my negligence now. Seeing ahead became an art. By leaning forward over the steering wheel, I could extend my focus beyond the drops of water to the road in front of me. But if I sat back, I could see nothing beyond the blur of greasy water thickening on the windscreen. It was an uncomfortable drive, therefore, with my neck cricked back like a cyclist's, but I would get there in the end.

At one moment I thought I saw Howard's Mercedes swim up behind me, but without a wiper on the back window of my car it was hard to be sure. I was driving a Mini, a car so low on the ground that I could rarely see more than a fraction of any car behind. If it was indeed North, he seemed to lurk behind in my blind spot like a spy.

How like him, I thought.

Why did I think it was like him? What evidence did I have, beyond his enigmatic silences? Then suddenly I remembered the doorbell, the evening after our first session together. The shape of him through the glass was indistinct, and I had been unable to see anything through the peep-hole because he had covered it over, but it must have been Howard. I had been so sure it was him. He had hidden from me then, too.

The memory of my fear was like the secondary tremor of an earthquake.

So I was right to feel frightened after all, I told myself. My instincts had been right. And if they were right – since there's no hard evidence to trust, just suppose my instincts are evidence enough – then Howard is following me now.

My heart lurched. I glanced in my rear-view mirror. Wasn't that his car? My imminent death at his hands seemed to loom up from the tarmac in different guises. A crushed car or a strangled throat, a swollen river corpse, a suffocated weight, a hanging manikin.

I drove off the motorway at the next junction and circled the roundabout twice. His car, if indeed it had been his, didn't follow me. As I returned to the motorway on the slip road I scanned the passing traffic for some view of him, but saw nothing remotely resembling his car. I doubted my instinct now as surely as I had fleetingly trusted it.

I came off the motorway for the second time at Salisbury. Once parked, close to the cathedral, I studied the map. I didn't know how I would find the place. I had no house name, number or road, nor even a village to guide me. I had a vague notion of its whereabouts, but the web of minor roads which threaded their way through that area was so dense that I could only despair. Or hope for incredible luck.

By the time I arrived, the day was almost dark. A cold light shone out from the kitchen window, so uninviting that I dreaded my task. What value was any further investigation now, frightened and lonely as I was? Wouldn't I just distort anything I learnt? I wanted to turn my car around and head straight back for London.

I waited a while, reassuring myself. I could see the old man hovering over the Aga, doubtless preparing some concoction for his cat. I thought I could smell it from the road. Would I give him a terrible fright, turning up like this out of the blue? Or would he be half-expecting me?

I got out of the car, into what was now only a slight drizzle. The air smelt so good. I remembered Howard's 'Ah' as he had breathed in the fresh air of Richmond Park. How I had loved him then. How safe I had felt with him at that moment of recognition.

This recollection soothed my agitation somewhat. I stretched my aching, car-compressed limbs into their original shape, my neck making something of the same noise as Bill's.

I walked up to the front door as confidently as I could, to deceive only myself that all was well.

I rang the bell and waited. I remembered from our previous visit that the old man was slow in answering the door. I walked around the front of the house to the kitchen window to see if he was aware of a visitor, but plainly he hadn't heard the bell. He was oblivious, pottering to and from the Aga with a smile. Perhaps he had a radio on, or perhaps he was just rather deaf.

Either way, I decided to leave him to his cat food a while and take a walk. I was enjoying the country air and wanted to snatch all I could before dark. At least I had found the place. I could relax a little now, after so much insanity.

I looked around me at the West Country hills, and a deep feeling of sadness overcame me. I was thinking of Howard, of his growing up in that particular landscape with that particular view. I ached for him, in spite of myself. He awoke in me a feeling that had lain asleep all my life: a feeling of significance.

And in that moment, just as I am told it will at my death,

my life seemed to play before me like a movie that starts so well and features such stars and yet goes nowhere at all. Were we all in this pointless journey together, or was it my unique destiny to fail? To merely exist amidst a series of unconnected events? To have no purpose, to affect no outcomes, to simply pass through life like an idle passenger? I would do something worthwhile, I told myself, and I felt better then, with this secret promise nestling inside me like hope.

Standing on the doorstep for the second time that evening, waiting for the old man to answer the bell, I fancied that I saw a shadow flit past the side of the house. Was it a shadow? Some movement, anyway, although it was so dark now that I might have imagined it. The old fear returned as suddenly as it had left. The thud of my thumping heart was beginning to wear me out. I felt like someone forced, after an all-too-brief reprieve, to ride the same roller-coaster again.

'Come on . . .' I urged under my breath, pressing the bell long and hard.

But still the old man didn't appear.

When I dared to look again at the side of the house, there was nothing to see. I supposed that a cat or bird or any wild thing might cast a moving shadow there. And if not, why, then I had seen nothing, it was fancy, no more. Night-time and fear will always combine to deceive the eye, to play havoc with good sense.

One more long ring on the bell and a couple of knocks on the door with my knuckles, and at last I heard the unmistakable sound of bolts being pulled back.

With the door-chain firmly in place, the old man asked, 'Who is it?' through a chink of light.

'It's me. Mo. Remember? I came to visit – a couple of weeks

ago.' No response at all. 'With Howard North? Don't you remember? Just a fortnight ago.'

I hoped for some recognition, some form of welcome. But when his face did finally peer out from the light, he seemed hostile and afraid.

'What are you doing here?' he barked, the astonishment bright in his eyes.

'Can I come in, please?' I whispered somewhat urgently.

He glanced down the drive, seeming as nervous as I was, as though expecting to see something very particular.

'What's the matter?' I asked.

'Come on in, then. Quick.'

He opened the door wide so that I could pass him, then closed it fast and firmly behind me. This done, he sighed with slight relief.

'What on earth is going on?'

'I might ask you the same question, my dear. What in heaven's name induced you to return, when my instructions were perfectly plain?'

'Your instructions?'

'*Stay away!*' he suddenly shouted, as though I were approaching a bomb about to explode.

We stood in silence for a minute or two, both of us baffled by his outburst. And then he seemed to be listening, above his own pulsing fear, for some evidence of the danger that he had implied.

I had the sense that we were somehow infecting each other with a mild hysteria that could soon get out of hand. I wanted to laugh. We were behaving absurdly for two rational grown-ups.

He eyed me warily.

'Something amusing you?'

'I'm sorry. I don't mean to laugh,' I apologized. 'I'm just — nervous, that's all.'

As he calmed down slightly, I sensed the same seriousness in him that had emerged towards the end of my last visit.

'I should think you are nervous,' he nodded gravely. 'Very nervous indeed.'

There was something immensely sobering about the way he said this. The steady sanity in his voice suggested a superior knowledge, as well as a greater wisdom by far, than I would ever possess.

I was about to ask him what exactly he meant, but he put a forefinger to his lips and with his other hand beckoned me to follow him. At the door of the living-room he made me pause, while he went inside and drew the curtains. Then he invited me to sit down beside the fire.

'You're wet,' he said. 'Come. Dry yourself. Nice and warm.'

He shut the door behind me.

Silence.

I expected him to say something, to offer some explanation, but he just leant deliberately against the door, lost in his own thoughts, as if I wasn't there. I felt impatient, but I restrained myself and tried to relax instead. Just as I was beginning to feel quite hypnotized by the flames, he suddenly asked me a most unlikely question.

'What have you done with Kittie's locket?'

'Kittie's what?' I pretended bewilderment.

'You know perfectly well what. I'd like it back, please.'

'Back? I don't know what you mean.'

'I'm warning you.'

'What are you warning me of?'

A feeling of panic seized me. Who was this man?

'Have you ever known murder, my dear?'

So here was the true psychopath, I heard myself think.

'I asked you a question. Please answer me.'

His question brought to mind the old tramp in Bloomsbury, struggling across the road, waving her white stick at my car. The moment at which the knife must have gone in became vivid now, as if I had actually seen it. A vicious effort of strength against the struggling life of her limbs. Surely Howard could not have done the same to his own mother? Surely no one could? Her sudden collapse jolted me back to the present. The terrifying immediacy of death.

'Yes, I believe I have. Known murder.'

His eyebrows betrayed his surprise.

'Nasty business, isn't it?'

'Are you threatening me?'

He laughed at this. I felt increasingly angered by his change-ability, which I perceived as calculated to deflect and control everything I said.

'I might be, mightn't I?' he said. 'And then again, I might not.'

I decided to meet his tyranny with a tyranny of my own.

'When I came down here with Howard, you spoke to me as if you knew me.'

'Did I?'

'You whispered to me behind his back. You seemed very scared. You told me that you couldn't find something. What was it that you couldn't find?'

'I don't know what you're talking about,' he said coldly.

'Yes, you do. Don't lie.' I paused. 'That other woman. The one who was so sure of herself. The one like me. I suddenly thought I knew who she was.'

His face seemed to freeze, in absolute terror.

'Have I said something wrong?'

He was looking beyond me now, at the curtains behind.

He mouthed his next words at me without any voice at all, but accompanied them with gestures: *Don't* (one hand making a dismissive gesture away from him) *say* (the same hand opening from a fist at his mouth) *any more* (both hands making a scissors cut across each other).

I realized that someone was listening to our conversation, though who or why I knew not, that they could not see us, and that plainly it was they who were the danger, not he.

I nodded to reassure him that I understood. My lips were sealed, I indicated, drawing an imaginary zip across my mouth.

Despite the evident danger we were in, I felt relieved that I was no longer alone.

'Are you feeling warmer, now?' he asked kindly.

'Much warmer, thank you.' I found some significance in his choice of words, as if 'warm' was to reassure me of a kindness and integrity that he couldn't otherwise show.

'Good.'

'I love real fires,' I said lightly. 'At home we only have one of those fake coal-effect fires because you can't burn real coal or wood in town.'

'Real fires are nice, aren't they?' he agreed, drawing the conversation to a close.

In the ensuing silence I wondered where the listener was. Had I, as I had suspected, seen a human shadow after all? What was that strong draught I could feel? Was one window slightly ajar? And why had I been made to wait at the door while Rolf closed the living-room curtains? There must be someone outside. Someone who had threatened this frail old man – with murder, perhaps? Someone who knew about the locket and wanted it back at all costs.

Had the old man actually seen me find and steal the locket,

and then rather stupidly let slip what he had seen? And if so, to whom?

My obvious suspect was Howard. It was so obvious, in fact, that I tried to think of other possibilities, despite my fear. Howard was too big for us.

I tried to guess which window was ajar, having decided that the outside was the most obvious place to hide. But the heavy velvet curtains, which the years had faded from a rich gold to a mouldy yellow, gave nothing away.

'Shall you be staying the night, my dear?' the old man abruptly inquired.

I tried to read some instruction from his expression but found nothing. I shrugged but he continued to look straight at me, stony-faced.

It occurred to me that the listener could now, unaccountably, see us both quite clearly. Or could they only see Rolf? None of the curtains in my eye-line had moved. I spun around on the sofa to look at the curtains behind me. I saw a last settling ripple as one fell back into place. I thought I also saw a glimpse of blonde hair, but that was too unlikely. What would Kate be doing out there?

The old man raised a disapproving eyebrow and shook his head. But he said:

'I can't think what you hope to see behind you, dear girl. This isn't a pantomime.'

'Sorry. I felt a draught.'

He nodded and smiled, but then his face froze again.

'I'm afraid you probably did. These windows haven't had any attention for years. They're practically falling apart.'

We sat in silence for a while. I was trying to think what to do. If only the listener *was* Kate, I would have no hesitation in simply opening the curtains and asking her what the hell she was playing at. But of course it wasn't Kate. Kate was in London, and Kate was a lot of things, but she wasn't quite mad yet. Even jet-black hair would probably appear blond with the warm living-room light falling on it through the yellow curtains. I must assume the worst. I must assume that Howard is out there now, dangerous and murderous, and after the locket I had found.

So if I left for London now, how safe was the old man? Did his well-being depend upon my being present or absent? How could I find out?

'Perhaps, since you weren't expecting me, I ought to leave you in peace.'

'As you wish.'

He seemed slightly dismayed.

'Unless . . . I wouldn't want to inconvenience you . . .'

'You wouldn't. Not at all.'

'In that case, if I could stay just for tonight . . . I've packed a few things in the car . . .'

'Do you need them urgently?'

I sensed from his question that retrieving them at this stage would not be advisable, although I was anxious to secure the locket. If it was such a vital clue, I wanted it on my person, for safe-keeping.

'No – I don't really,' I said. 'I can leave my teeth for one night!'

He smiled.

'If I were you, I'd just settle right where you are – it's the warmest room in the house. Doze off by the fire.'

I suddenly had this terrible fear that he might be setting me up. He might be about to leave me alone in the room, with the murderous Howard outside the open window, just waiting for a moment alone with me.

145

'I'm feeling quite paranoid,' I said, hoping that he could reassure me somehow.

'Paranoid?'

'I don't know anything about you. For all I know, you might be a murderer.'

I felt that I could say this quite legitimately, without endangering either of us, since we had already spoken of murder fairly openly.

He laughed.

'I'm serious. You were certainly trying to frighten me earlier.'

'And so I was, my dear. You needed frightening. Young women are ill-advised to turn up at remote country houses where lone men reside, at any time of day, let alone at night-fall.'

There was no comfort to be gleaned from these words, utterable by anyone anywhere, although not in quite the same formal English he chose.

I wished I believed in angels. I would have summoned one then. I wished I had secret access to Bill, that I could somehow bring him careering down the motorway with policemen on motor bikes, in cars, in helicopters overhead. Like the husband he never was.

'I shall probably kip down here myself if you don't mind, my dear. I don't tend to venture beyond that door much after nine o'clock.'

'By all means,' I said warmly, sighing with relief. 'What's happened to Kitty.'

'She's outside killing things. At this time of night. If she's lucky.'

This sentence wasn't the most conducive to sleep, but he offered nothing further, and was soon snoring loudly in the chair opposite me. He dribbled slightly over the pink blanket that virtually strangled him, its colour more appropriate to a baby of six months than to a tired old man.

I turned out the remaining light and watched the embers glow. When they finally extinguished themselves, I closed my eyes and replayed the evening's events again in my mind's eye.

I didn't sleep at all. At about midnight I heard a car start and saw its headlights peep through the curtains. I leapt up to have a look, fearful that it was my own car being driven away, but I could see very little in the dark. All I could see was that it was not my car. My bright yellow Mini was plainly visible. It sat, like an ally keeping watch, where I had parked it earlier, whereas this car was so dark in colour that it almost seemed not to exist between its head and rear-lights. As it drove past the window I could see only that it was a long car, not a hatchback, and not an estate. A Mercedes would fit the description well.

15

I woke to the sound of birds, the light of the morning sun and a cup of Darjeeling, although which stirred me first I couldn't say. I suspect it was only when the old man had drawn back the curtains and placed the porcelain cup by my side that I was aware of either sun or birds.

The sunlight was a welcome and soothing surprise after so much rain. I almost felt happy. But even the most wretched, dull day would have sufficed to shift my fear.

'Thank you,' I said warmly.

I looked up to smile at the kind old man but, to my horror, discovered that Howard North was towering over me.

My breath left me.

'What are you doing here?'

'I might ask the same of you.'

'I drove down last night.'

'So I understand,' he said sharply, but then, changeable as ever, added gently, 'Whatever were you thinking of? Driving down here on your own?'

'I don't know,' I said, confused by his sudden concern. I rummaged through my sleepy mind for some half-decent excuse.

His eyes searched my face for something. A clue? A betrayal? Or was it the same something he was always wanting from me? An emotional void? If so, it was the last thing I felt capable of giving him then. My feelings were like bubbling nectar waiting to be drunk.

'I just – I just wanted a break.'

'Home-life rather a strain, is it?' he replied curtly, sharp again, as if dismayed by the struggle he had seen in my face.

'It's been easier,' I admitted.

'I can't say I'm surprised.'

'No, I'm sure you can't. It's exactly what you planned, isn't it?' I snapped.

He didn't show any alarm at my irritability. Perhaps he was satisfied that my anger was sufficient proof of my honesty.

'You followed me, didn't you? I thought it was you,' I said.

'Why on earth would I want to follow you?'

'You tell me.' But he didn't. 'What are you doing here if you didn't follow me?'

'I do own this house, Mo. I have every right to be here.'

'Do you?'

'Of course I do. "Only son and heir", that sort of thing.'

'You didn't kill her for this house, did you?'

It was out before I had even thought about it, let alone intended it. A look of such intense fury overcast his face that I feared for my life. But it passed in a split second, like a bird flying high in front of the sun. He then became very calm and clear and, more like a police officer than a criminal, he began to fire questions at me. They came so fast I thought I might confess to a murder myself.

'Who have you been talking to?'

'My husband.'

'And who has he been talking to?'

'Kate, I suspect.'

He clenched his jaw with icy control.

'And what has he learnt from Kate?'

If I tell him, what will he do, I wondered.

'I asked you a question, Higgs.'

'Apparently you murdered your mother.' It sounded so absurd that I thought he might laugh. 'You were the chief suspect, at any rate.'

He stared at me.

'I see,' he said, and paused. 'And you believed him? Of course.'

'No, I didn't. Not necessarily.'

'Didn't you?'

His face was suddenly open, like a grateful child's when someone at last takes his side against authority.

'I found the thought intolerable. But if it's the truth, then I hope you'll . . . own up to it. What else can you do?'

He sank down on the sofa beside me suddenly, his face buried in his hands.

'I was coming to this, Mo . . .' He was frowning, his hands combing through his hair. 'I wanted to tell you the whole story, that's why when you kept asking me during that first session what had I done to my face – remember that?'

'Yes.'

'And I said, let me tell you in my own time, in my own way, from start to finish. Do you remember that?'

'Yes, I do.'

'You see, I was coming to this.'

He stared ahead in perplexity, whatever plans he had nurtured now thwarted.

'I couldn't just start with a murder and expect to be understood, could I?'

'I don't know,' I said, flatly.

'You wouldn't have believed me, for a start.'

'I might have done.'

'The risk was too great,' he said adamantly.

There was a long pause.

'At least you feel remorse,' I offered, to comfort myself more than him.

'What for? What are you saying? I thought you understood?'

Understood what? Murder? I wanted to shout, but checked myself in time.

Every sudden change of his mood seemed to threaten my life.

'I didn't do it, Mo.'

'You didn't do what?'

'I didn't –' he stopped abruptly, glaring at me like a man betrayed. 'Dear God, must I spell it out? Even to you?'

'Yes, I'm afraid you must,' I said.

'I did not kill my mother, Mo. What possible motive could I have? I loved her! I don't want this monstrous house. It's a bloody albatross. I'm stinking rich as it is. What do I want another bloody house for? I was keeping her, for God's sake!'

'What do you mean, you were keeping her? You hadn't seen her for two years.'

'I was sending her cheques. So she could pay bills. She was utterly dependent on me. I'd kept her in money for years.'

'Perhaps you didn't want to keep her any more,' I suggested impetuously.

'Well, I wasn't, by the end. She wouldn't be kept.'

'Why not?'

'She'd all but disappeared. I couldn't get the cheques to her. No one knew where she was. She wasn't cashing them.'

'So where was she?'

He stood up and walked over to the window. Four birds

suddenly arrived from nowhere and danced in front of it, in an unlikely, uniform line.

'They say that when somebody dies, birds often do this – dance and sing like this – as if the spirit were revisiting.'

When he turned back towards me his face showed such grief that I hated myself for ever doubting him.

'I'm sorry,' I said.

'Yes,' he replied, looking through me.

'I didn't mean to be cruel.'

He smiled, a mild, benign smile of resignation, as if I had been his last hope and I had run out on him.

I felt I could have laid down my life for him then.

'How can I help you, Howard? What can I do?'

He looked surprised.

'Nothing. You're very kind. Nothing. You've done enough. You've tried.'

'I haven't done anything. I've let you down, that's all.'

'Nonsense. You've done your very best. I know you have.'

'How can I help you? Tell me!'

He paused, studying my face, as if ascertaining the appropriateness of what was to come.

'If you really – really want to help –' He paused in shyness, his face colouring slightly. 'You see, you mustn't fall in love with me, Mo.'

Of all things. That.

'Why not?' I could feel my cheeks burning.

'If you do, you can't help at all. You mustn't love me.'

He looked out of the window again, as if to avoid my gaze.

'The trouble is, the real difficulty is, that I could fall in love with you. Which would make it doubly hard for you. Because in my heart I would very much want you to love me, too, that's the difficulty. Because I'd end up trying to make you love me

152

in spite of myself, in all sorts of unhelpful ways which I can't seem to control. I think perhaps I'm already guilty of this. But you mustn't love me, you see. However much I want you to. You absolutely must not.'

Even the back of his neck seemed to be blushing as he looked out over the fields.

How could I ever not love him?

We remained silent until I dared to ask:

'What if I already do?'

He turned from the window and gazed at me with such longing that I thought we were both lost.

'Do you?' he asked.

I looked away, unable to withstand his eyes.

'I hope not, for both our sakes.'

He came back to the sofa and sat down beside me, taking my hand in his with all the tenderness of love.

'You see, you must use your head, Mo. Examine the facts. I'll tell you everything I know, if you'll promise to seek the truth. Seek it out, like water. Look for the truth. Not for my answering love. Just for the truth.'

He spoke with all the urgency of a man sentenced to death. The sentence was emotional, I realized, not literal, although he may have felt so lonely by then that suicide presented an alternative hell.

I was reminded, by the content of his words, of Neville Hoare's writings. A passage about courage which I remembered well echoed him word for word, almost. The essential point had been that any search for the truth, be it spiritual or physical, needed courage above all, the courage to face every possibility.

'I'll try,' I said. 'I really will try.'

'Thank you,' he said.

I sipped my tea, which was unbearably sweet.

'Any good?' he asked anxiously.

'A little sweet. But very warming. Thanks.'

'The old boy made it. Wasn't sure if he'd added sugar or not. He seems to add sugar to absolutely everything.'

'What's that burning smell?' I asked, suddenly aware of it.

'Toast, I think. He's been cursing the toaster all morning.'

He hovered over me a while longer before deciding against further conversation.

'Charcoal and marmalade suit you for breakfast, then?' he said, grinning as he left the room.

A short while later the old man came in, balancing a tired brass tray which he rested on my knees. Howard stood behind him, smiling to himself.

'Toast and marmalade, my dear!'

'Thank you. How delicious.'

'A little burnt, I'm afraid. Blasted toaster – got no automatic pop-up, has it? Flipping useless thing,' he muttered at Howard.

'Charcoal's good for you,' I offered.

'I hope it isn't quite charcoal, my dear,' he said politely but very firmly.

Howard pulled a conspiratorial face at me.

'Oh, no. I didn't mean – I meant just the edges being a little – well – burnt. Not really charcoal as such.'

Silence.

'More tea?' he asked, finally.

'I'd love some without – without so much sugar, if you're – making some.'

'Very well.'

He pushed past Howard like a piqued old woman whose whole sense of herself lay in the reception of her breakfasts.

'Oh dear . . .'

'My fault, I think,' said Howard.

There was an awkwardness between us as soon as we were left alone. The shared intimacies hovered around us like the visiting birds, unforgettable. And the way through this dense silence seemed suddenly impenetrable, like picking a path through the tangled roses outside.

Howard took the initiative.

'When all this is over, perhaps we'll be able to . . .' but he trailed off into silence.

'Able to what?'

'Perhaps we'll be able to love each other a little, I was going to say.'

The words ran over me like caressing fingers, their tips finding every secret, sensitive place.

'But I was forgetting your husband,' he said.

16

Howard spent most of the day digging the pond. It had only been a small pond, but it took some digging. He attacked the earth with ferocity, his newly purchased spade gouging out great lumps of soil like a greedy spoon at a thick chocolate cake. There was little I could really do to help with my heavy spade, but what I could do I did.

The knowledge of the locket, tucked away in my suitcase, was beginning to trouble me. I was determined to give Howard this reward for his efforts, this precious clue, but I was reluctant to admit to its theft. I preferred to return it to the mud of the pond, where it could be miraculously happened upon all over again. And yet the double dishonesty of this after his demand for the truth was more troubling still. Why had I held on to it in the first place? He would be as offended by my secretive suspicion of him as he would by my dishonesty. What could I do? I had gleaned all I could from the locket; there was nothing to gain from holding on to it. Perhaps I could simply tell him the truth, and risk a moment's wrath. He'd hardly kill me.

'I'm just going to take a break, Howard.'

'Right.'

'Anything you want?'

'Nope.'

He was barely conscious of me, such were the demands of his mission.

During the morning he had watched my every move – in

anticipation of what, I did not know. He wouldn't even let me retrieve my suitcase from the car, insisting that I looked fine as I was and that my teeth would survive one day's negligence. Was this the beginning of my gradual demise? From one day's negligence into a thousand of self-abandonment? I had borrowed his mother's hairbrush, feeling it was not altogether right to do so, and otherwise I obeyed him. Something was almost broken in me, surrendering. By the afternoon, Howard seemed confident of his control of me. He relaxed his vigilance. I was able to go to the loo without his finding some spurious reason for accompanying me. I therefore assumed that it might be safe to collect the locket at last.

I was also very keen to catch the old man on his own. I wanted to ask him a few important questions before the locket left my safe-keeping. Not least, what on earth had happened the previous evening that had so tyrannized him. Although it was true that my fear of Howard had diminished substantially, I was still profoundly uncertain of him. My fear had shifted. I was no longer personally afraid of him, since he seemed to pose no immediate threat to me, but there was undeniably a darkness lurking within him that might threaten somebody. He himself had made it my business, my duty, even, to find out the truth.

The old man gave a terrified start when I came upon him in the kitchen. He was all nerves still, I realized. His apparent calm at breakfast had misled me into believing that Howard was not a man he feared. I had assumed that all was well again, that whatever had been amiss the day before was amiss no longer. Now I realized that I was wrong.

'What's the matter?'

'Tea, my dear?' he asked, in flat denial of my question and his fear.

'Tell me.'

He eyed me warily, as though expecting some impending violence.

'Nothing to tell.'

He looked away from me, out through the window at the drive.

'You can trust me, you know,' I said gently.

'Nonsense.'

I found his reply baffling.

'Why so sure?'

'Howard thinks he can trust you –'

'Does he?' I was flattered, in spite of myself.

'Not for me to put him right, but I know he can't.'

'I'm sorry?'

'I saw you.'

'Saw me? Saw me what?'

'Where is it?'

He meant the locket, of course. What did he know? I had been so confident of his pliability, and yet he continued resolutely to defy me. I had slipped back into stereotyping, which classified this old man as 'docile', or senile or fragile, or anything ending in '-ile'. In fact he was more alert and shrewd than any of us. He would never be any man's fool again, as perhaps he had been once or twice in his life. He was living on his wits as though he had only just come to them.

I was aware for the first time that he might be a part of this plot, or intrigue, that he might have some stake in it.

'I'll give you some advice –'

'You've given me enough.'

'Give me the locket. Get in your car. Go home. Leave us alone.'

'Who's "us"?'

'You have no idea of the danger you're in.'

'If you'd only be specific about it instead of threatening me, I might have some idea, mightn't I? Who knows, I might even do as you suggest.'

He seemed to be thinking about how much to tell me. He was narrowing his eyes as an artist sizes up a model before painting her. But I felt that he couldn't actually see me; he lacked the necessary insight to grasp my soul. Whereas Howard already had it in the palm of his hand.

'Who are you, Rolf?'

'I'm nobody's fool, my dear, I can assure you of that.'

'I didn't think you were.'

'Least of all yours.'

'I'm flattered,' I said drily.

'Don't be,' he said. '"Flattered vanity/Leads to insanity."'

'That's nice. I like that,' I said, aware that these two short lines headed the first chapter of Neville Hoare's book, which was sitting in the suitcase in my car. Had he broken into my car, rifled through the suitcase, perhaps even found the locket, and was he now telling me so?

'Does it matter where the locket is?'

'A great deal.'

'Why?'

'Do you have it on your person now? Give it to me. Please. Now.'

'You must tell me what's going on,' I said firmly, using a certain authority that I reserved for occasions like this. It often got me what I wanted when all else had failed.

'I can't,' he said, responding in kind. 'Not possible.'

Authority was not going to work with the old patriarch that he was gradually revealing himself to be.

'Why not?' I asked. 'What harm can it do?'

'A great deal of harm.'

'Listen, Rolf. I don't want to cause you any harm. But I can sense that something is seriously wrong. I want to help.'

He seemed so profoundly wary of me that no reassurance, however sincere, was likely to satisfy him.

'I know your kind,' he said cynically, testing my goodwill with this inference.

'My kind?' I asked, testily.

'Your cunning, feline kind – stealing people's secrets from them.'

'I thought you liked cats?' I said flippantly, ashamed of the truth of what he said. The thieving truth.

'I do.' He paused and smiled suddenly, changing direction with characteristic dexterity, like something feline himself. 'Too much for my own good.' And he winked improbably.

The sexual implication of this wink was too awkward to contemplate. And yet he might once have won me for a day. How hard it must be to relinquish one's sexual power to old age, after years of mastery, like a useless tool. He might even have won my heart twenty years ago, attractive and astute as he was, rather like Howard, but he would have broken it, too, I felt sure. I thought of Howard's mother and her broken heart. And then something suddenly dawned on me. I looked at the old man again, studying him closely as he waited for me to say something, and I realized who he was. It was the eyes that gave him away. The sadness around his eyes. Just like the photograph.

I chose to keep the realization to myself, for the time being at least. The more he thought I knew, the less he was likely to reveal.

'What are you afraid I might do,' I asked, 'if you tell me?'

'Who knows? People can do terrible things, can't they?'

He looked strangely haunted suddenly, as if by some memory, like a man traumatized by the horrors of war, who suddenly remembers some gruesome torture inflicted upon him.

'What terrible things are you thinking of?' I asked.

He didn't answer me.

'Were you ever married, Rolf?' I inquired, out of the blue.

'What sort of question is that?'

He was indignant. I felt duly ashamed of my bluntness.

'I don't know,' I mumbled. 'I just –'

'What has it to do with you whether I was married or not?'

'I'm sorry. I didn't mean to pry.'

There I was again, I thought, asking too many questions too soon. In fact I realized that I didn't want to know too much about Rolf, even if he was the man I thought he was. I wanted only the information relevant to the case. It was Howard's story I wanted.

What a task it seems to be to find out the truth, I conceded wearily. Are we all so secretive, or is there something truly hideous buried here somewhere?

'I have to ask you something less personal, then,' I said determinedly.

'How refreshing,' came his dry reply.

'That woman you mentioned –'

He seemed to bristle immediately.

'The one who looked so like me?'

'Yes, I know who you mean,' he replied curtly.

'Did she do something – anything – terrible?'

He looked at me uncertainly, wavering on the precipice of the truth.

'I would have to tell you everything, right from the start. It wouldn't make any sense, otherwise.'

No short cuts, in other words. Like father, like son.

Suddenly Howard was standing in the doorway, still and silent in his soft woollen socks, unannounced by either step or breath. How long had he been there?

'Is she harassing you?' he asked, trying to sound unconcerned.

'You shouldn't creep up on people like that,' said Rolf.

'Just wondering where my assistant digger had gone . . .'

'Any joy yet?' I asked, trying to appear guiltless of any intrigue with the old man.

'Only in seeing you,' he said, with unlikely ease. He must have heard Rolf's ungainly attempt at flirtation and was mocking him.

'Tshh . . .' hissed the old man fiercely.

'Take it on the chin, Rolf,' Howard teased. 'Some of us can still get away with it.'

'Just!'

'And some of us just can't!'

The banter was light, but barbed with sharp, possibly lethal thorns.

'What are you hoping to find out there anyway?' asked the older man irritably. 'You're wasting your time.'

'What the bloody hell do you think I'm hoping to find? Evidence, of course. One tiny clue that proves I didn't . . .'

He shut up as suddenly as he had burst forth, his brow furrowed like one of the ploughed fields outside.

'Proves you didn't what, Howard?' I asked.

'You know what, Mo. Didn't kill her. Proves I didn't kill her,' he said.

'Does she know?' Rolf barked, looking at Howard like an astonished deer.

'Do I know what?'

The old boy looked at me as though I were a tiresome child, always in the way. Then he looked back at the other adult in the room.

'Howard? She doesn't know, does she?' he asked again.

'She knows something,' he said.

'How much do you know?' the old man demanded of me, his face close to mine.

'How much don't I know?' I asked Howard. 'Because I get the feeling that you're hiding a lot from me still. I get the feeling you're deceiving me.'

'What have you been talking about?' Howard asked the old boy irritably.

'I haven't said anything, I swear,' he answered.

Rolf seemed momentarily frightened of North. It was as though he didn't know quite who to be frightened of, but he knew that someone was very much to be feared. Howard, or Kate, or even me. Or was there someone else involved in this whole intrigue?

'I suddenly had the sense that you two were related,' I said provocatively, making the most of their joint anxiety.

They looked at each other for a fraction of a second that left me in no doubt.

'Yes, I've had that sense sometimes, too,' Howard deflected ingenuously. It was neither a truth nor a lie.

'You should check out your family trees,' I suggested.

'Yes . . . perhaps we should . . .' He contrived to be preoccupied, lost in his thoughts again.

'You said "evidence",' I continued, unwilling to let him withdraw. 'As Rolf said, what exactly are we looking for out here?'

'You must have a better idea than anyone,' Rolf accused me pointedly.

'I'm not looking for a body,' said Howard, thankfully ignoring Rolf's indiscretion, 'if that's what you mean.'

'Why not?' I asked. 'The body could be there, couldn't it?'

'How does she know about the body?' Rolf shrieked in dismay.

Howard ignored him. 'It isn't in there, Mo. It was made to look like an accident. She was given a proper burial. Her grave is up at the village church.'

'How do you know?'

'Because –' Howard glanced at the old man – 'because – I remember.'

'But you didn't remember before, did you?' I asked.

'What is this? Some kind of interrogation?'

'You didn't, did you?'

'No, I didn't.' He paused and sighed. 'I didn't know then. I have subsequently done my research. Now I do know. They would have been idiots to bury the body themselves. Can't you see that? Far too obvious.'

'So how did you find out they'd buried her at the church?' I asked.

Another furtive glance at the old man.

'I walked up there and had a look.'

'So there's a gravestone with her name on it, is there?'

'Not her actual name, no.'

'What, then?'

'For God's sake, Mo! I thought you trusted me?'

'Why should a few questions imply that I don't? I'm trying to find out the truth. Trust would, I feel, obstruct that objective process, don't you think?'

He smiled for a moment, almost pleased with me.

'Very well.'

Again he looked at the old man, shrugging slightly.

'Are you two in cahoots?' I asked, feeling slightly paranoid.

'Kahutz?' asked Rolf. 'Where's that?'

We all managed a laugh of sorts, mine rather more constrained than theirs.

'No, we're not. Not in any conspiratorial sense,' said Howard. He took a deep breath. 'God, it's so impossible, this. If we'd only stuck to our bloody therapy sessions, Mo, we'd have covered this ground weeks ago. The trouble is that more keeps happening before I've even told you the essential story itself.'

'Well, perhaps it's time to tell me the essential story.'

'Yes, it is. Of course it is. Only things are getting somewhat urgent.' He furrowed his brow again. 'I'm under quite a serious threat, that's the trouble. And so is – so is . . .'

'Rolf?' He didn't even nod. 'From whom?'

'Too many questions, Mo. Too many questions. Remember your training. Trust your client's process, eh?'

'But you're not my client, Howard.'

'No, I'm not, that's true, I'm not. But I still – I feel rather as though I am, still.'

'Then let's have a session, shall we? Tell me the story. You're expecting an awful lot of me if you think I'll just come along for the ride.'

'Of course.'

He fell silent, his head bowed.

'What's the problem?'

'The almighty risk is the problem, Mo.'

17

He took the risk, or at least a part of it. A part of the whole. It seemed a substantial enough part at the time.

He chose the village church as his venue, driving me there in his grumbling car. 'Not her again,' it seemed to be muttering.

The church stood at the top of the hill, attacked by fierce winds. Like its teachings, it turned the other cheek.

'I'm really biting my tongue, Howard – it's frantic with questions.'

'One thing at a time,' he replied firmly.

The Mercedes mowed over the mud and grass of winter.

He pulled up the hand-brake and climbed out of the car. I remained glued to my seat. He opened my door.

'Come on, Mo.'

He stroked my cheek, his warm hand kind to me. I took it in my own cold hand, and kissed it. Then I let it go, conscious of the danger of love.

'I'll show you the grave,' he said, 'just so you believe me.'

'I do believe you.' But he was already striding towards the edge of the graveyard where no stones were.

'Where is it?'

He lifted a mass of brambles to reveal the tiny, heart-stopping size of her neglected stone. Her gravest of gravestones.

'This is hers.'

He had to pull away the brambles and ivy to read the inscription.

'I deliberately covered it over again last time – just in case – I don't know why – just cautious.'

It had certainly been completely hidden until he had uncovered it. Even the tiny mound in front was nothing but a bed of nettles and grass.

I can't bear it, I thought. I can't bear to look.

'What does it say?'

He read the words with a flat, numb voice, too grieved to intone what spoke so well for itself.

> 'The shortest life is best,
> The longest sleep most sweet.
> Blessed be thy rest,
> Until we next shall meet.'

I had to fight to hold on to my objectivity, with her little body lying so close.

'Whose words?'

He looked at me, his eyes narrowing thoughtfully.

'Not Katherine's, surely?'

He shook his head.

'Rolf's?' I ventured bravely.

'My father's words.'

This wasn't an answer, but it wasn't a denial either.

'Very beautiful words,' I said kindly.

He nodded.

In the church, sitting in the front pew, he said:

'I could almost have faith sometimes, just out of necessity, just because the brain collapses under the weight of too much to understand.'

'There's a lot, isn't there?' I mumbled, keen to get started on the 'too much to understand'. I was too curious, too perplexed now, for any further delay.

'It's all right, Mo. I'm coming to it,' he said, reading my thoughts.

He took a deep breath, inhaling the musty air of the church, of the wooden pews and the heavy stone and the damp cold cloth of the cushions and tapestries. Wasn't there also the smell of the huge Bible itself, an old book-bound smell of history?

'You can't lie in a church, can you? Even if you have no faith. The tyranny of childhood wraps its rules round you.'

'He is your father, isn't he?' I said, unable to restrain myself any longer.

He smiled at me and shook his head patiently.

'You've got a lot to learn about therapy, Mo.'

'He is, though, isn't he?'

He nodded.

'He says he is.'

'Don't you believe him?'

'I think so.'

'Why would he lie?'

'I don't know. People do. Don't they?'

I felt that he could see my lies as if they were written on a long list, like an open scroll in front of him.

'Isn't he familiar to you at all?'

'No. I have almost no memory of him. Kittie never spoke of him. No photographs or letters, no belongings, nothing. It was as if he never existed. I remember after Cassie's death, when he left us, Kittie was frantic to find some locket that had his picture in it. But we never did find it. He took everything else.'

The locket. How increasingly important it was. I thought of the man locked in with her. Anton Chekhov's eyes. The likeness was now so obvious, I wondered how I had ever missed it.

'When did he come home?'

'Only very recently.'

'Where from?'

'He went back to India after Cassie's death. Or so he says. He was always in love with a beautiful Indian girl, even when he married Kate – I mean – Kittie. Katherine. It wasn't acceptable to marry Indian women then. Natives. So he married my mother instead, to keep the peace. To keep up with his family, with social expectations, all that bollocks. He was wretched about it. And Kittie was wretched, too, of course. She loved him. After the drowning, he left. He went out and married the Indian girl. Didn't get a divorce. Just married again, under a different name.'

' "Rolf"?'

'That's right. Rolf!' He laughed affectionately. 'Of all the names to choose!'

'So he's been in India ever since then? All those years?'

'In the main.'

He paused, thoughtfully.

'I would go into more detail, only it's – well, it's his life to tell or not, isn't it? I'll fill you in on what's relevant.'

'Fair enough,' I agreed.

And the rest, I schemed, I can get from the horse's mouth.

'I suppose he felt that he'd married a kind of witch,' he said.

'He had, hadn't he?' I quipped.

He glared at me, as if daring me, like an eclipsing sun, to look straight up at him.

'I'm sorry. I'm so sorry. That was a stupid, facetious, flippant thing to say.'

He looked away, accepting my remorse.

'She wasn't a witch to me. Far from it ... I loved her profoundly. Do you understand? Profoundly.'

'Right.'

'Try to understand,' he said, clearly unimpressed by my response. 'Profound love is profoundly forgiving, Mo.'

'Yes, I believe it is,' I said.

'It enables you to forgive the most vicious acts of revenge. The most violent crimes. Understanding is only part of it. The real key is love.'

'Howard, I don't need a lecture on love. I just need to hear the truth.'

'Quite right. Quite right, Mo.'

'So it was Rolf who told you about Cassie's burial?'

He hesitated, flinching slightly.

'Amongst other things.'

'What is his real name?'

'William.'

'William? How funny.'

'Why?'

'It's my husband's name. Bill.'

'No,' he said categorically, 'William or nothing. Why do you think I was christened Howard? So no one could shorten it. He hates shortened names. Whereas Bill was doubtless christened Bill. Wasn't he?'

'He wasn't, actually, no.'

We fell silent. Unspoken tensions began to pollute the air.

'Have you been married long?' he asked abruptly.

'Ten years. Is that long?'

'Does it feel long?'

I laughed at this. The for ever it had been.

'Sometimes,' I admitted.

I studied the lines of his face.

'Have you ever been married?'

'Mo,' he warned. 'One thing at a time.'

'I want to kiss you,' I said quite out of the blue.

'Don't, would be my advice,' he said.

We were caught unawares for an instant.

'Come on, then,' I said brusquely, breaking the silence like a diver in a still pool of blue. 'Tell me things!'

He smiled, almost laughed at my efforts to resist.

'I will, I will, I will!'

But then he looked at me so longingly that neither of us could say a word.

'You mustn't do this, must you? North.'

'No. I know.'

He stood up and walked over to the altar and waited like a bridegroom there.

If he had ever married, I thought, this was as likely a place as any for him to seal his fate.

'He only told me yesterday what actually happened to Cass.'

Yesterday? I wondered. When, yesterday?

'Does he know?' I asked.

'He knows what happened to her body.'

'And he told you over the telephone, did he?'

'No.' He seemed surprised by my question. 'He told me in person.'

'But you weren't here yesterday.'

'I was.'

'When?'

Had he been that shadow, after all? That frightening threat?

'I came down very late. Or early. In the early hours of the morning, in fact.'

'Funny time to travel.'

'I only found out rather late last night that you weren't at home.'

'So? Does that mean you have to follow me?'

'Yes, I'm afraid it does.'

'Why?'

'Because we're all in danger, Mo. You most particularly.'

'That's reassuring to know. Thanks for the warning before I got involved.'

'I couldn't warn you. I'm sorry.'

'How did you know I'd be down here?'

'I guessed.'

'Am I so transparent?'

'Sometimes.'

'How did you "find out" I wasn't at home? You didn't ask Bill, did you?'

'No, I didn't ask Bill. I drove past your house.'

'And rang the bell? And covered up the peep-hole?'

'No.'

He seemed saddened by my fierce interrogation of him.

'I'm just seeking out the truth, North. Staying objective.'

'I know.' He paused. 'I'll tell you the truth. I came down very late. The old boy was still up, pacing about like a ghost – he was white as a ghost, certainly. He'd had some terrible shock –'

'What shock?'

'I don't know. Somebody had threatened him –'

'Not you?'

'Me? Why me? Threaten my own father?'

'You weren't very fond of him last time you mentioned him, were you? He'd ruined your mother's life, by all accounts.'

'Yes, he had. He did. And he'd be the first to admit it, too,' he almost shouted, the anger shining in his eyes.

'So you found him pacing about . . .' I said calmly, trying to pacify him.

'Yes. I found him pacing about.'

He paused.

'And?' I persisted. 'What then?'

'And. Then. He all but collapsed in my arms.' His face betrayed him, the emotion quivering like lapping water, blown.

'A reunion? Of sorts?' I suggested.

He looked at me as if I understood about as much as an officer in the SS.

'He believed me at last,' he spat at me contemptuously.

'Believed you?' I echoed, as detached as I could be.

'He believed I didn't kill her.'

'Kill who?'

'God, Mo! You're the limit! You're so fucking blunt!'

'You've asked me to be. Please answer the question, North.'

'My mother! Who else? I didn't kill my mother. All right?'

'Well, forgive me, but there was the initial question of Cass's death, too.'

'I didn't kill either of them!' he shouted.

'You're sure of that, are you?'

'Yes, I'm sure of that,' he said, mimicking me.

'Why is it so hard to say, then, if you didn't kill either of them?'

'This is like being in court . . .'

'Answer the question.'

'You'd make a good barrister, Higgs.'

'The question, North.'

'I find it so hard to say, Higgs' – his voice was lethal as steel – 'because they're both fucking dead. I'm suspected of killing them both, so I can't fucking grieve. I've never grieved a fucking

173

thing in my life. It's all in me still. It's ... hard ... to ... say.'

We were silent for a long, long time. My thoughts chased each other about in my head. My feelings rose and fell like a lover's body, up and down. I waited for the whole morass to settle inside me before I dared anything else.

'It's getting dark,' I said finally.

'Figuratively speaking?' he asked.

He was still standing at the altar, waiting for her to arrive. I walked over and took his hand.

'You're going to be all right,' I said. 'You'll have your time to grieve.'

He nodded, not really believing me. Then he wrapped his arms around me, hugging me to him like a piece of flotsam in a shipwrecked sea.

'We've only just started,' he said.

During the drive back, he told me that Cassie's body wasn't in the graveyard at all.

'So where is it?'

'Rolf told me the truth last night.'

'Do we have to go on calling him Rolf?'

'Yes, we do, I'm afraid. Very methodically.'

'Why?'

'Because if he's William, then he's Cassie's father and he's the man who disappeared two weeks after her death – which seemed accidental, but was it? In other words, he was a suspect, too. Primarily because he did disappear. And he still is, all these years later. A suspect.'

'They lie in wait, don't they, these cases?'

'They seem to. The irony is that if he'd stayed in the country, there wouldn't have been an inquiry at all. As it is, what with Katherine's murder and me being a suspect, the case is now open again, like everything else about my family. Open house. Open to scrutiny.'

Open, I thought, like a wound, raw and gaping, the dressing ripped off.

'So what did happen to her body?'

He stopped the car outside the house.

'Apparently,' he began, his face whitening with nausea, 'my mother – my mother dug it up again – after the funeral.'

'Oh, no.' My imagination leapt. 'What did she do with it?'

'She sent it – she wrapped it up and sent it . . .'

'Where? Not to India?'

'That's right. To India. To my father. All wrapped up in sacking and cloth. In a square wooden box.'

'Jesus . . .'

'It was boats in those days. You didn't fly out there. Nor did the packages. So by the time this sweet-smelling gift finally reached him, it stank unimaginably. Of dead, rotting flesh.'

I couldn't find any words.

'He's never recovered from it. Would you? Your own best-loved child?'

As we approached the house from the drive, the old man's face smiled out at us from the kitchen window.

How different he looked to me now. How desperate his smile seemed.

18

The day dragged on, filling up with new wonders.

As I washed up after supper – if the word 'supper' can be used to describe two hard-boiled eggs with burnt toast – the old man suddenly grabbed my arm. Howard was somewhere else in the house and I feared that the old boy was choosing his moment to make a pass at me.

'What are you doing?' I pleaded, as he pulled me towards him.

'Has someone stolen it?' he whispered urgently in my ear.

'Stolen what?'

'The locket!'

If only to prove the impossibility of this, I almost confessed that the locket was in my car, but then I remembered that he had probably searched my car and had failed to find it there. He had no proof that I had it at all.

'What locket do you actually mean?' I asked innocently.

'Tsssh . . .' he hissed at me. 'Be serious. Someone has broken into your car.'

'You broke into it, didn't you? Somehow. At least I assumed you did.'

'I had a look, yes. But someone else has also broken in.'

'What! In this remote place? I don't believe it!'

'And they have smashed the window in –'

'Oh no,' I moaned wearily, thinking of the time and money that it would take to fix.

'Whereas I simply used your key –'

'When did you simply use my key?'

'While you were washing your face.'

'How dare you?'

'Just to see if it was there.'

'And was it there?'

'I couldn't see it,' he admitted, 'but I wondered if you had hidden it very cleverly. You must go and check immediately that it's still there.'

'I don't have a locket to hide anywhere very cleverly. I imagine it's just an ordinary burglary. I assume my suitcase has gone?'

'No, your suitcase is still on the passenger's seat. It has been opened, however. Someone has looked through it very thoroughly.'

The suitcase that Howard had insisted I leave in my car. Why?

'Shit!' I exclaimed, exasperated by this news.

'Howard wants it, of course.'

'Wants what?'

'The locket.'

'Is that who you're suggesting has broken into my car? Howard?'

'No, no. Goodness no. He hasn't the faintest notion that the locket has even been found, let alone hidden away.'

'Why haven't you told him of your suspicions, if you're so convinced I've hidden it from him?'

'Are you serious? Why haven't I told him that you've deliberately deceived him, lied to him? Would that be helpful, do you think?'

'Possibly, wouldn't it?'

He was angry, almost indignant, at my suggestion, and punished me with silence.

'Why do you want this locket so much?' I asked, but he still wouldn't answer. 'So you can give it to Howard yourself? Like a caring father at last? Or so you can destroy the evidence that implicates you in some way?'

He flinched, though at which question, I didn't know. For this very reason a skilled detective would ask only one thing at a time, I rebuked myself.

'He's told you, has he?' asked the old man.

'What?'

'He tells you everything.'

'He's told me you're his father, yes.'

The old man became very grave.

'If you tell anyone –'

'I won't.'

'He thinks you're a veritable safe when it comes to secrets, doesn't he? He trusted your clever twin, for all the good it did.'

The way he said 'clever' somehow highlighted my dull unsubtlety.

'You mean Kate?' I asked, my envy of her undisguised.

His expression grew suddenly stern.

'I don't know who you're talking about,' he said, imploring my discretion with his eyes.

I was reminded of illicit trading, the thickness of thieves, conspiracies.

'Neither do I,' I said complicitly. But he looked doubtful. 'You can't stop me asking questions, Rolf, but I won't answer them to anyone else.'

'What questions?' he asked.

'Were they lovers, then? Howard and Kate?'

'Tssh . . .' was his evasive answer. I thought that this probably meant 'yes'.

'Did she threaten you? Last night?'

'Did Kate threaten me? Why would she threaten me?'

'She wanted the locket, didn't she? Why were you so frightened last night? Who frightened you?'

'Questions are dangerous things –'

'Was Kate here last night?' I demanded.

'Did you see her here last night?' he asked logically.

'I might have done.'

'Do you think you did?'

'Possibly. Yes.'

'Then perhaps you did,' he said, shrugging indifferently.

'She used to come down here,' I said, determined not to let him escape, 'with Howard. Didn't she?'

'Occasionally, yes.'

'And you were living here.'

He didn't answer.

'How come you were living here?' I asked.

'This is my home. I bought this house myself, many years ago.'

'So you came back to England to claim it? Once you knew Katherine was dead?'

'Good heavens, no. What a shocking suggestion.'

He sat down at the kitchen table, as if he no longer trusted his legs.

'Where's Howard gone?' he asked warily.

'I don't know.'

'Check the corridor.'

I did.

'He's not there.'

He relaxed visibly.

'I came back to find them both, that's why I came back. To make my amends. I didn't intend to stay, but I wanted to make my peace.'

'So you turned up here and . . . ?'

'And nobody was here. Eventually I broke in, fearing the worst.'

'The worst?'

'I half-expected to find two rotting corpses here, for some reason . . . But there was nobody at all. A lot of post, addressed to Katherine. Bills, mostly. The various services had all been cut off – the telephone, electricity, gas. Even the water. I was about to report her absence when Howard arrived at the door, with your – with Kate.'

'So you didn't report her absence?'

'We did. Most certainly, we did. But nobody could find her – not for months. When they did eventually find her, of course, she was dead.'

'How awful. For you.'

'For Howard. Awful for Howard. He had finally broken free of her terrible possessiveness, only to be possessed again by this . . . this . . .'

'This what?'

'This – whatever it is. Something possesses him.'

I had the feeling that he knew exactly what it was, but didn't wish to say.

'I'd better check my car, hadn't I?' I asked rhetorically, leaving him alone in the kitchen.

Outside, under a clear moonlit sky, I discovered that the locket had gone.

19

Bill was out when I got back, early the following morning. There was nothing unusual about his being out, and I hadn't warned him of my imminent return, but his absence made me curiously uneasy.

Although I'd left Wiltshire abruptly and with some urgency, once in London I felt immobilized by indecision, like a driver at a junction where several roads beckoned me.

Perhaps I could tell Bill the intrigues I had discovered? But then, he would always take Kate's side. And how should I approach Kate? What if Kate didn't have the locket? How could I investigate anything anyway, with my modest experience, largely acquired vicariously through Bill?

I flicked through the opened mail on the hall table. Brown envelopes mostly. Containing red reminders. It used to be me who took care of the bills, paying them with meticulous regularity and promptness out of our joint account. It was my job. My pathetic contribution to our lives. And I even took pride in my efficiency, routine as it was. It was a symbol of my grasp on reality. A post-stillbirth resolve.

And now? Was this an overt rebuke? Had he planted this evidence of my negligence where no one could miss it? Least of all me.

'Why can't he pay the fucking things himself?' I said out loud.

I kicked the table, ridiculously, as if it were the enemy, in sympathy with Bill. It shuddered in surprise and let fall, amongst other things, an itemized telephone bill.

On picking it up, I glanced over it and noticed several long calls to what I knew was Kate's number. I had hardly phoned Kate in the last three months, and certainly not at any great length. These calls had to be Bill's. In spite of all my suspicions, I still felt betrayed. How I longed to be surprised by him, to discover a true change of heart behind his puffing hot words about saving this marriage of ours. Refreshingly, the discovery troubled me only for an instant.

What troubled me far more was the thought that she might have information about Howard, that she was in some way more intimate with him than I would ever be. Now why should that be worse than Bill betraying me? The thought troubled me so intensely that my whole equilibrium was thrown. Envy and rage surfaced in equal measure inside me. How dare she travel so close to the heart of him? When I was stumbling still, somewhere near the borders of his land?

I paced about in futile agitation before throwing open the french doors into the garden, where I began to attack various overgrown roses with a vicious pair of secateurs. The thorns ripped at my skin in self-defence.

Later, exhausted and somewhat tranquillized by this cathartic butchery, I had the car window replaced by emergency glass. And then I waited for Bill to come home. I waited like a sentinel, checking the time, responding to every sound.

At about seven o'clock I heard a car park outside the house. I jumped to the window to see if it was him. But it wasn't. It was North. The headlights of his motor car switched off like eyes closing wearily. Howard looked at my own small car, and then around him – for Bill's? – and finally up at the house. Then he climbed out and stood on the pavement.

So this is him when he's watching over me, I thought to myself. He can't see me staring straight back. The lights aren't on. He probably thinks I'm out. Or does he think I'm dead?

I opened the front door and shouted to him.

'What on earth are you doing, North?'

He jumped.

'God! Don't do that to me!' He caught his breath. 'I'm keeping an eye on you, what do you think?'

'I'm perfectly all right. I don't need a bloody bodyguard.'

'Are you on your own?'

'Isn't everyone, in the end?' I asked facetiously.

He laughed at this, half-bitterly.

'I mean –' he said in a loud whisper, 'is your – is Bill with you?'

'I don't know where he is.'

We stood looking at each other like teenage sweethearts.

'Come on in,' I said. 'If Hugo doesn't mind waiting.'

'Hugo?'

'Don't you think he's a Hugo?' I said, indicating his car.

'Oh. Him.' He looked at his car as if for the first time. 'Maybe ... Hugo or – Maurice? Something rather élite and pleased with itself.'

He approached me shyly, one awkward step at a time. On the top step he said:

'Aren't we friends at least?'

'Of course we're friends.'

'I hope so.'

'Of course we are.'

'You mustn't just leave me like that.'

'Leave you?'

'Suddenly you'd just gone, Mo.'

'I had to. Sorry.'

'Why?'

'Because. I did.'

I turned away from him into the house. He followed me, closing the door firmly behind him.

What am I doing? I thought. A feeling of terror rushed through me. What am I doing inviting this suspected unconvicted murderer into my home?

I stood suddenly still, facing him.

Let me at last know the truth, I thought. Even if I die of it. Kate knows, doesn't she? Let me know, too. Let me know more.

'So why am I in such danger that you have to keep this vigil over me?'

'I can't tell you.'

'Why not?'

'Trust me.'

'Trust you? Why? Tell me the truth, please. I need to know the truth.'

He paused, as if thinking about telling me.

'I don't like it that Bill's not here,' he said, looking around him suspiciously.

'*You* don't like it? What about me? I've been betrayed by him for as long as I can remember.' I waited, splitting my sentence in two, for any first reaction from him, before I added, 'He's been having an affair with Kate.'

It was definitely this second statement that pained him so.

'With Kate? Why Kate?' There was a wild look in his eyes. 'What makes you think he's having an affair with Kate?'

'I know,' I said lightly, as if Kate were anyone. Then I picked up the telephone bill, still lying on the hall table, and pointed to her number. 'Kate's. I haven't been calling her.'

He looked down the long list of calls. He made no effort

184

to disguise his feelings. Perhaps they were too profound. He turned away from me, his arms across him as if clasping an ache in his heart, like an illness in him. He leaned against the wall for support.

'No,' he moaned. 'She can't do that . . .'

'Why can't she?' No response. 'Howard?' I wasn't sure that he could even hear me. 'Why can't she? What is it to you?'

He looked at me, finally, as if I'd only just arrived, as if I'd stolen upon him in the fullness of his grief like some merciless journalist.

'She can't . . .'

'Of course she can,' I said.

I noticed that I was enjoying watching his illusions about her shatter at last. My pleasure shamed me.

'Come and sit down,' I said kindly. I began to pity him, and, with this softening of feeling, I also pitied myself. 'Let's sit down next door,' I said, guiding him into the living-room, on to the sofa.

He sat shivering while I lit the coal-effect gas fire.

'She's unbelievable,' he said.

I sat beside him, holding his hand like a mother comforting a child after his first nightmare.

'She's very important to you, isn't she? Our Kate,' I said, understandingly.

'She's very dangerous.'

'Dangerous? Kate?' This was the last thing I expected him to say. 'I love her,' yes. Or, 'She promised me,' yes. But 'dangerous'? Did she represent the great danger I was in?

'You mean dangerous – to men?' I said, trying to make sense of it.

'Dangerous,' he said, 'to women, Mo.'

His eyes focused on me. I nodded wisely, believing that I understood.

'Sure. I see. I mean, I do see, of course. If she's stolen my husband from me. I see how her –' I was going to say 'charisma' but just couldn't bring myself to – 'how she can easily threaten women like me. The ordinary ones.'

He caressed my cheek with what felt like pity.

'It's OK. I'm used to her showing me up,' I said, laughing self-effacingly.

'You're unique, Mo.'

He leaned towards me – to kiss me? Only in a fraternal way, I was sure, but at that moment a brick – a plain red brick – crashed through the window of the living-room.

'What the fuck . . . ?'

Howard leapt up and closed the curtains fast. He stood rigid, alert, breath held. Finally he exhaled and walked slowly to the other end of the room, where he closed those curtains too.

'What the fuck was that?'

He nodded, as if approving my fear, like a director approving an actor who has finally mastered a scene.

'Now do you believe me?'

'You're not saying that was Kate?'

'I'm not saying anything. I'm saying you're in danger, Mo. Please take care.'

'What should we do?'

'Nothing. Yet. Wait.'

We fell silent. He seemed to be listening for any further threat. I was reminded of the old man on that frightened, frightening night. Had the same danger tyrannized him? Even down to the brick? I remembered the fierce cold draught I had felt in the living-room. But the next morning? There had been no evidence, had there?

'Can you hear anything?' he asked.

'No.'

'Good. Neither can I.'

He sat down again.

Was that it? Weren't we going to do something?

'What's going on? Please! You have to tell me.'

He took a deep breath.

'It's not fair, North.'

'Is anything?' he asked rhetorically.

'We usually have it within our power to be a little fairer than life.'

'I love you,' he said, in a way that couldn't possibly mean love as I meant love. 'Your high principles!'

He beamed fondly at me, and then studied the coal-effect fire.

'People's lives hang in the balance every time secrets are revealed.'

This sounded rather melodramatic to me, but I didn't say so. Let him tell it, I thought, as theatrically as he likes, only let him tell it at last.

'But I will tell you,' he said, as if reading my mind.

He narrowed his eyes in concentration, choosing where to begin.

'I've told you I was an adopted child, haven't I?'

'You have.'

'There's no simple way to tell this story, Mo. I always balk at it, like a horse at the last fence – or the last fence but one . . .'

'Have you told many people, then?'

'What was that noise?' he said suddenly, pricking up his ears.

'What noise?'

'I thought I heard a noise . . .'

'I don't think so,' I said.

Pause.

'So, you've told a few people, have you?' I persevered patiently.

'I've told only two people in my whole life. I took forever to find the courage. It's harder every time. Perhaps because the reaction is always so strong, so – disgusted. And the more I esteem a person, the more difficult it is. I fear your opinion immensely, it seems, what with your high principles . . . your right and wrong, black and white. I've been trying to tell you for weeks . . .'

'There's no hurry,' I said, suddenly nervous again of what he might reveal, what crimes he might be answerable for. It has to be murder, I thought. What else could it be? And then I thought, it could be something else. It could be rape, or paedophilia. It could be necrophilia. It could be anything.

'We were lovers, my mother and I.'

But that? No. I hadn't allowed for that.

He wouldn't look at me. He stared ahead of him, straight at the fire. I was glad of this. My face must have betrayed my shock. My bewilderment. Even my contempt. The unutterable revulsion I felt.

My mind ran over this love affair like a dog on a scent seeking out the creature's lair. Her bedroom, the garden, that whole secret house to themselves. I could see them doing it, she seducing him with the sweet reassurances of a mother's love, massaging his virgin muscle into her. Aaah! His ecstasy! His re-entrance into the womb that never bore him. Mother. Body beloved. Those heavenly eyes all over his nakedness. Discovery of her most secret, urgent parts, hungry for him all, every inch of him hers, she whom he loved so profoundly still.

'You're horrified,' he said, finally looking at me. He could read the expression on my face. Blatant as nudity.

'Was it her idea, or yours?'

He didn't answer me.

'Surely it wasn't yours?'

He shook his head, though more in dismay at me than in denial of my words.

'Sorry,' I said. 'I'm just – I'm trying to understand.'

'But you don't, do you? You don't understand.'

I couldn't pretend I did.

'Nobody ever does.'

He turned away again, as if it was he who was disgusted now.

'It's not – it's just not within my experience,' I said, trying not to shame him any further than I had.

'That's apparent, Mo.'

We fell silent, each in our different worlds, our estranged terrains.

'It must have been a lonely secret to bear,' I offered, struggling towards empathy.

'We had each other,' he answered, simply enough.

'But later, as you grew older. Or even just at school?'

'I didn't go to school,' he said.

'Why not?'

'My mother taught me – from an early age. She taught me everything.'

'Yes, evidently she did,' I said, unable to resist the quip.

He glared at me.

'Sorry. You know me.' I tried to laugh it off.

'I'm beginning to know you,' he said soberly.

'Tell me more,' I encouraged him, in a gently inquiring tone.

'She didn't teach me all the way through. By "everything" I just mean the basics, just the three Rs.'

'I see,' I said, trying to sound sincere.

He glanced at me suspiciously before continuing.

'When I was ten – or was I eleven? – she employed a tutor for me. Theo, he was called. Very clever. Handsome, too, well-built, very strong . . . someone to emulate. He was like a surrogate father to me – I was almost in love with him. I longed for him whenever he went away. A crush, you'd call it these days.'

'You had a crush on him?'

'Yes, I did,' he said defensively, 'the same way every adolescent develops a passion for one of his own, before he ventures towards his opposite.'

'Sure,' I said affirmingly, puzzled by the strange coy phrasing he used.

'Then one day in the woods – I must've been about fifteen – I came upon him, or rather, I came upon his backside. It was incredibly white, I remember, and muscular, clenching and releasing, thrusting and mounting, up and down, back and forth. I was mesmerized by the savage rhythm of it. He was fucking my mother. Of course. Who wouldn't? A remote country house, a woman like her, lonely and hungry for love? I hated him from that day forth. He didn't see me. Only my mother saw me. She saw my distress.'

'Sure,' I said, persuading him on.

'She almost – she . . . She seemed to smile at me. Did she? I don't know. All I know is, I suddenly felt this incredible urge for her, this urgent desire burning in my groin. I wanted to do what he was doing to her. Somehow, despite all its horror, its violent savagery, she seemed to be enjoying it. It seemed to be allowed. She allowed it. And she allowed me, invited me to follow, if only because she – she smiled so sweetly at me.'

'Sure,' I said again, not trusting myself with any other words.

'That evening in bed – we'd always shared the same bed, since my father left us . . . That night I – I put her hand on

190

me. I was bigger than I'd ever been. It was a gift – like a gift for her. It was hers. I told her, "It's yours, it's mine for you." And she took it. She received my gift. Rapturously. I mean that. With rapture. She took me.'

'I see,' I said. And I did see. I saw that to take him with rapture was too easily done.

'That was how it began. And how it went on. We lived as lovers. In the end we lived – more or less – as man and wife.'

'You actually married her?'

'I thought I was adopted, Mo.'

'But were you?'

'I don't know. I don't know any more.'

'What's made you doubt it?'

'My father, of course.'

He looked to me for some comfort then.

'Poor Howard,' I said.

But he frowned instantly. Here was the same mood-swing I'd encountered in him before, always when he was at his most vulnerable. His sudden and total frustration with me, like an infant's rage at its mother, when I failed to deliver whatever he needed most from me.

'Don't pity me,' he said. 'I don't want your pity, Higgs.'

'I'm – sorry. I don't mean to . . .'

'I loved her. Profoundly. That's not pitiful.'

'No,' I mollified him.

I thought it was pitiful, though, just as my love for him was pitiful. Love was more often pitiful than noble, I was beginning to believe.

There was another sudden crashing of glass, this time outside.

Howard leapt up again, fingering a crack through the curtains whilst scarcely disturbing them, like a detective in an old black and white film.

'Damn it!' he almost shouted.

'What is it?'

'Someone's smashed the window of your car.'

'What? I don't believe it! Not again!'

'Again?'

'I've just had it fixed. Today.'

'Was it broken before?'

'While I was with you. In Wiltshire. I assumed you knew. Someone broke in.'

'No. I didn't know.'

He sat down again beside me, sighing wearily.

'I assumed the old boy would've said something.'

'He knew, did he?'

'He discovered it.'

'He makes me nervous. There's so much he doesn't say.'

'Like father, like son,' I suggested.

He looked at me, as if admonished by the accusation.

'Yes. Very possibly.' He paused. 'Where was I, then?'

You'd just got to the bit where you first screwed your mum, I heard myself think but, thankfully, not say.

'It makes me so jumpy, this tireless tyranny,' he said.

'It's pretty frightening,' I agreed.

'It's best to ignore it if we can. Not show any fear.' He paused in thought. 'Marriage. That's it. That's where we were. You asked me, while we were in the church, if I'd ever been married.' He paused again, wary of me. 'Well, we did marry, Kittie and I. In Italy. Tuscany. Very secretly.'

This gets worse and worse, I thought. Please, no, they didn't have a child?

'And then, later, after Lizzie, someone else wanted to marry me. Henrietta, she was called. A big sweet girl. She wouldn't leave me alone – kept badgering me. I never loved her, but

Kittie was furious. Frighteningly so. She scared her off by telling her about Cassie – for my own benefit, she said, because I was plagued. Cursed. Because women risked their lives by being drawn to me. She said only she could ever survive me, because she knew the truth. She called it my anger at her.'

'And was it?' I asked nervously, having seen that anger myself.

He paused, thoughtfully.

'When I first met you – at Kate's party – Kittie was still alive. I hadn't seen her for two whole years, but she was still alive. As I later discovered. Certainly I had little reason to think she wasn't. A few days later, just before I asked for your help, she was dead. I asked for your help because I needed to understand. Why was she suddenly dead?'

Despite his methodical delivery, I could tell that he was close to tears, reining them in.

'I needed to know if I'd done it. She couldn't tell me any more. She was dead, dumb-dead. If I had done it, then I'd finally done it to her.'

He was choking on his feelings now. They rose in his throat like vomit.

'They all thought it was me. As you know. But they couldn't detain me. Not enough evidence. They held me overnight – no longer . . . But they're still after me.'

'I sort of assumed they were.'

'And one person in particular is still after me. Tirelessly. She wants her revenge, she's trying to frame me. She'll stop at nothing,' he almost shrieked, the frenzy in his eyes beginning to frighten me. 'I understand it now, you see.'

'Uh-huh,' I said, wishing I did.

'I didn't kill her, I know. I didn't kill anyone. The old boy's explained it to me. Things are clearer than ever. I think I can finally see what's been happening, what the pattern is.'

'The Plague?'

'The Plague! That's right. The Plague. I see how it plays itself out.'

'So Kate is after you? I assume it's Kate.'

He looked at me guardedly.

'Kate is after me, yes.'

So many questions were inside me, pushing for a voice, but I knew from his manner that he had said enough. I suggested instead that he might like something to eat or drink, or he might just like to sleep.

He chose sleep.

'Just for a short while,' he said. 'Just here is fine.'

He was sound asleep in minutes and stayed asleep most of the night. I switched off the lights and kept watch over him.

My own mind was as restless and sleepless as a wild animal's, hunting, or hunted, or both.

20

A sharp winter sky brought an early light to the house. The barren branches of trees were drawn across its blank canvas like dead fingers. The room was thick with confidences. I opened the curtains. The broken window let in the cold air. Howard stirred, but then slumbered on. He seemed to be mine, lying there sweetly asleep like a trusting child.

He pained me. I was part of him now. He had let me in through an open door, where I had stood knocking for weeks. He'd even shown me around. At my own request. And now? I wanted to go home. Like a child at a fun-fair who was hungry for new thrills, the House of Horrors had finally proved too much. But I couldn't leave. I was in too deep. I couldn't get out, even if I wanted to.

I looked around me at the disarray. The shattered glass, the unpaid bills, the pile of rose-cuttings outside. I needed some order again, some ordered ordinariness, if I was going to continue on the strange dark journey ahead.

I woke Howard.

'You'll have to go, I'm afraid.'

'Mmm?'

'Just in case Bill comes back.'

'Yes.' He rubbed his eyes sleepily. 'Yes. Of course.'

'I don't want things to get any more complicated.'

'No.'

Pause.

'Tell me what Kate's trying to do,' I asked.

'Eh? Kate? Do?'

He was still scarcely conscious. I gave him some coffee and swept up the glass. Then I telephoned a glazier. They would fix it straight away, they said. Then I paid a few bills. Before dealing with the rose-cuttings, however, and before the glazier came, I wanted Howard out of the house. I also wanted some questions answered fast.

'Howard –'

'Yes. I'm going,' he said, standing up at once.

He looked at me searchingly, warily.

'It's OK, I'm not about to kill myself,' I said lightly. 'I've just got things to do.'

'I understand,' he said.

Do you? I wondered. Do you understand that, because of you, my life is changing irreversibly?

'Tell me, Howard, if I'm to help you – what does Kate want from you?'

'I – I don't know.'

'Don't lie to me,' I said firmly.

His eyes again focused on me like the lens of a camera. A portrait photographer's eyes, seeing into my soul.

'Revenge. Is what she wants.'

'Why?'

He wouldn't answer.

'What have you done to her? . . . You must tell me, Howard. It's very important that I know.'

'Why? Why on earth should you know?'

I thought of the locket. Shall I tell him? Do I dare?

'You need to know that she's dangerous, Mo. Leave the rest alone.'

'All right, then,' I said, 'if you won't explain your affair with her –' he bristled visibly – 'then at least tell me this: how can she frame you?'

'Because she knows about Cassie –'

'How?'

'Because I told her. How do you think?' he replied irritably.

'Why did you tell her?' I persisted.

'That's not your business, Mo.'

'Very well,' I said impatiently, 'if that's how you feel . . .'

I was filled with furious curiosity. I wanted every detail of their love-affair elaborated upon. He could sense this, I knew.

'It's neither relevant nor safe for you to know about our relationship.'

'If that's how you feel . . .' I repeated.

'That is how I feel,' he replied adamantly.

A long pause.

'So she knows about Cassie's death?'

'Yes. And that I felt some uncertainty. About whether I'd done it or not. If she can produce any evidence that I did do it, that's going to weigh fairly heavily against me in court, in the case of my mother.'

'I thought they regarded each case in isolation?'

'Well, that may be. But if the jury get wind of it – they only need a whisper of it – even if they're told quite clearly to disregard it, they won't. They'll heed it. Wouldn't you?'

'Quite possibly,' I admitted. 'What evidence could she find?'

'I don't know. Probably none. But she could plant it. Or she could find the evidence I need, the evidence that could prove I didn't do it. She's already threatened the old boy, demanding that he tells her if we find anything. She uses the lowest tricks. She's told him she'll expose him for who he really is – for my father – and thus implicate him in the two murders, if he doesn't keep her informed. If she gets hold of any evidence that could help me, she'll destroy it.'

'She wouldn't do that, surely?'

'She would do anything.'

'She would even plant false evidence?'

'Believe me,' he said, 'she would do anything.'

'And what is this evidence you need, to prove your innocence?'

'It's just a locket. My mother used to wear it. I think I mentioned it to you.'

'Yes,' I said, too fast. 'Yes, you did.'

'It was lost during the event of Cassie's death. It just might provide the essential clue. And then again, it might not. But until I find it, who knows?'

I thought of the broken chain. The struggle by the pond.

'Really, above all, I need to prove it to myself. I can't take my father's word for it. I can't take anyone's. I have to see it for myself.'

An uncertain, desperate hope had invaded his eyes.

'I just want to be sure. Or I can't go on living with myself.'

Had I let it go, careless idiot that I was? The one clue that would save him.

'So. She seems to hold your life in her hands.'

'She'd like to. She doesn't yet.'

Oh, but she does, I thought. She does, she does, she does. And it's all my fault.

We both sank into our thoughts as one sinks into quicksand, helplessly.

'What is it you have to do?'

'Sorry?'

He had summoned me back.

'You said you had things to do.'

'Yes, I have. And I don't want you following me. Please?'

'Then where will you be tonight? When it gets dark?'

'I haven't the faintest idea. Not with you, I hope.'

He flinched at this.

'I don't mean it. I just mean – I like to be with you, Howard, I just – I don't want a bodyguard.'

'You need one, Mo.'

'I don't. I can look after myself. And I can certainly defend myself against Kate. I've fought with her often enough.'

He sighed, exasperated.

'God, Mo, are you always this bloody stubborn?'

I thought of Bill's words: 'Be told.'

'Usually,' I said.

'Realize this, then, if you'll realize nothing else: schoolgirl fights aren't Kate's style any more. She doesn't play at this. Look at that brick.'

'What did she do, then, to Rolf?' I asked nervously, studying the brick.

'Enough said, Mo.'

He tweaked my nose and smiled. Then, impulsively, he kissed me full on the mouth, his warm hand caressing my neck.

'I need you.' He said. 'Badly. Be careful. Please.'

He left after that.

21

As soon as the window was fixed, I too left the house. I switched on the burglar alarm, just in case. I also took a small sharp knife.

Waiting at Kate's front door for her to answer the bell, I felt a hollow loneliness, like air, filling me up. I thought about Bill. I wondered if I'd find him there. I minded, at last. Suddenly and furiously. I dreaded the truth about the two of them.

How was it that Kate moved through each loved person in my life and stole them away from me unfailingly? Sooner or later. She was most often there before me, but sometimes after me, and always more emphatically.

When Cliff opened the door, I felt an immediate rush of relief. My ally. My fellow-sufferer. He stood there like a medieval knight, glowing with uncomplicated strength, a shining sword in his hand. He could cut us all free, untangled as he was in this thorny wilderness. He seemed to me, at that helpless moment, to be the answer to everything.

'Mo! You've just caught me. Walked in two minutes ago.'

'I was just – I was after Kate, in fact.'

'Kate?' How surprised he seemed. 'Kate's walked out,' he said. 'I thought you knew that? She's gone.'

'Gone?' I couldn't believe it. 'Where?'

'I don't know,' he said. He was putting the kettle on.

'She's not with Bill, is she?'

'I don't know, Mo,' he said. He searched my face. 'I imagine so.'

I let the news sink in. He put his arms around me, comforting as a big brother's arms. He smelt of clean shirts. I had never stood close enough to Cliff before to enjoy the smell of him. He had always been out of bounds.

'Let me make you some coffee,' he said.

I felt as though I had stepped into someone else's life. It was a curious and unfamiliar sensation. As though everything building up to this moment when I had come to see Kate, with a small knife in my bag, had not in fact happened to me. As though I had come here only to be with Cliff. To be reassured. To be taken in hand, by someone capable and strong.

'How come you're not at work?' I said.

'I've got to pick up the kids.'

'Who's looking after them?'

'I am,' he said. 'That's why I'm not at work.'

'But what about your nanny?'

'It's her day off,' he said.

'Oh, Cliff, I'm so sorry,' I said. 'I'm sorry for both of us.'

He was mixing the coffee beans in the grinder.

'Half-Continental and half-Colombian,' he said mildly, as if he hadn't heard me.

The noise of the grinder prevented any further conversation for a moment. I was glad of this. I watched the back of his neck, his cropped black hair cut sharp against his warm skin. Like Howard's. I could see the muscles of his back push out against his dark blue shirt. A sudden and bewildering desire to make love to him ran like a visitor through me. Was it Howard's story that was breaking down these boundaries for me? Or was it Kate's treachery? Or was it because Howard would not permit my love and it had nowhere else to go? Achingly unfulfilled.

'There's no need to be sorry for me,' said Cliff. 'We've always had an open marriage. It was a deal we made early on. There was always the chance that one of us would leave.'

I was shocked. He said it all so easily. He looked at me calmly.

'We were suffocating each other, Mo. She wanted too much. More than I could give. She wanted to own me. So we worked it through, and that's what we settled for. Open or closed was all she could take. No middle ground. We've kept out of each other's way ever since.'

'What about the kids?'

'They're OK,' he said. 'They never knew.'

'But what about your lovers, then? How did they cope?'

'Differently,' he said. 'Everyone is different.'

'Every lover, you mean?'

'Every person, Mo.'

Pause.

'Did you have many, then?'

'I suppose I've had many lovers in my time,' he said. 'I'm a child of the sixties, remember. It's not such a big deal for me to have sex. Do you want milk?'

I couldn't get the thought out of my mind, the desire for him out of my limbs. I didn't know what to do, where to place myself.

'Darling Mo, where are you?'

'Eh?'

'Milk? Or not milk? Simple question. Simple answer required.'

'Black is lovely,' I said.

He led me into their comfortable living-room, where a new portrait of Kate smiled graciously down at us. As I looked up at it, like a mortal at a god, I was seized by an intense, vehement hatred, such as I had never felt for anyone in my life. How dare she do all that she does and still smile down like a sweet, angelic muse, heavenly to all men? The hideous deceit of her beauty, that concealed such toxicity. How dare she?

'Funny old painting, that,' said Cliff, somewhat irreverently. 'Who did it?'

'That enigmatic character – what's his name? She's known him a couple of years . . . God, what's his name? North? Richard North?'

'Howard?' I said despairingly, but he didn't hear me.

'The guy who's supposed to have killed his own mum . . .'

'Yes. Howard North.'

'That's right. He did it.'

'Is he a painter, then?'

'I don't think so. I don't know what he does. Something in the therapy world. All very intense. He paints for a hobby, I think.'

Howard? My interest in the painting became instantly prurient. How had he seen her, when she sat for him? I looked for clues of their love. Her breasts were visible through her open silk shirt, the nipples firm and erect, as if excited by him. Her expression was fresh and wild, her skin porcelain-pure, her lips slightly parted for the smile – a distant, dreamy smile that deflected from the sinister depths of her chocolate-brown eyes.

'Like it?'

'Not really,' I said, admiring the skill but loathing the subject and all that it implied. So uncomfortably like me.

'I don't either. She looks like a psychopath.'

Cliff was so reassuringly simple. So wholesomely down-to-earth.

'Now if you were up there,' he said, suddenly behind me so that I could feel his breath, 'with your sweet breasts pushing out like that, I'd feel quite differently.'

His breath felt like Howard's breath, warm and soft. I looked round at him in confusion.

'Have I overstepped the mark already?' he asked.

'Possibly,' I said.

'You draw the line. The choice is yours,' he said. He was serious.

I smiled awkwardly and moved away from him. I sat down on the sofa, sipping my delicious coffee. Rich, dark, strong.

'Like it? My brew?'

'Lovely.'

This is Cliff, I told myself. Your old friend Cliff.

'Have I embarrassed you?' he asked.

'I think I've embarrassed myself!' I said, as easily as I could.

'I'm sorry. I just . . .'

He sat down beside me.

'Nobody's fault,' I said.

'You looked – you just look so – hurt.'

He was studying me with a concentration that he usually gave only to work.

'I'm all right,' I said.

'I want you, Mo. I can't help it. Sorry,' he said.

I breathed in his desire as if it were a summer's day. Fresh grass, warm hay, lilac, wisteria. The smell was so sweet. I could feel tears prick my eyes.

'What is it?' he asked softly.

'Nothing.'

'Tell me.'

'It's – it's just things. Things at home.'

'Bill?'

'Yes. Partly Bill.'

He caressed my cheek.

'I know,' he said, and although he almost certainly didn't know, I needed to believe him then. 'I know how it is.'

His hand travelled down to my neck, caressing the tension there.

'Is this OK? If I do this?'

'Do what?'

'Make a little love to you?'

'No, it isn't,' I said, battling with tears, baffled by this unexpected seduction, which I felt I had brought upon myself. 'It's not OK at all.'

'Fair dos,' he said easily, taking his hand away.

And yet the promise of a little love, of physical intimacy, a naked body, warmth, it was so tempting, too. I wanted it too much. I wanted Howard to make love to me.

'It's OK, it's lovely,' I said, closing my eyes.

His lips were warm and soft on mine already. Howard's lips. I kept my eyes closed and let Howard in. His tongue pushed into my mouth, penetrating deep inside, stirring my senses into a hungry need for him, a need for all of him, a need for his need of me, his desire of me.

He took my hand and let it caress his hardness. Howard's hardness. For me. His gift to me, pushing out against the cloth like an arrow poised in its bow, quivering in anticipation of release. I ran my fingers over its round, urgent tip, titillating it.

'Oh, God . . .' he murmured feverishly as I opened him up, his voice low and deep, vibrating through me like love. Like Howard's love.

I bent down over him and took him into my mouth. He moaned helplessly as he thrust himself in and out of me. Then he pulled me up and searched me and found me with his hands. I cried out but he stopped my mouth with a voracious, devouring kiss, one hand still playing below while his other hand climbed up to my breasts, stretching to take both of them at once. Then he kissed my neck, falling on it like a bloodsucker.

'Let me see you,' he said, kneeling down, unpeeling my clothes, layer by layer. He gasped with pleasure, his tongue burning me now, torturing me with the promise of his ultimate entry. I opened my eyes, blurring his features like a soft-focus lens, so that I could only see dark hair.

He laid me on my back so that I could see Kate and Kate could see me and I could think of Howard as I felt the wet round fruit of his love push its way into me. He moved fiercely back and forth, tearing off his shirt and opening mine, taking one breast in his mouth and biting the nipple hard. Howard's desire burst over me like the sun. Warm golden love. I came in waves, shuddering after him.

22

Afterwards, with the weight of his body like a corpse on top of me, I wanted to leave for ever. Leave everything behind. I had trespassed into a cold other world where the senses ruled, while the heart was ridiculed. I felt contaminated. Was it Howard's dark secret that had worked like a fever through me, hot and irrational? A disease of the mind, impelling me forward through obvious boundaries?

Like a refugee fleeing the status quo of my own country, I had come upon the guarded borders of another land, hostile and merciless, but I had crossed them as simply as one crosses a road, briefly hesitant, glancing just fleetingly from right to left and back. I didn't see what was coming at me. Until it was too late.

'What's the time?' asked Cliff, rolling off me like a lazy seal in the sand.

'Twelve-fifteen,' I said stiffly, pulling on my clothes.

'You no joke with me?' he asked, in an accent I had never found funny.

'It's a quarter past twelve,' I confirmed coldly.

'Shit.'

He stood up, dragging his trousers from his ankles to his hips and zipping them up. He bent down over me.

'Sweetheart, you were wonderful. I've wanted to do that to you for as long as I can remember.' His wet lips presumed themselves to be welcome on mine.

'I'm like one of those bastards you hope you only read about who leaves the instant the deed is done, aren't I? But I have got to pick up the kids.'

I could hear him saying this heartless sentence to so many less indifferent women than me, and I felt for them all.

'Did Kate have an affair with North?' I asked plainly, as if it didn't matter to me. I was staring at the portrait again.

'I wouldn't put it past her, would you? She's an anarchist. I mean, it's against the rules, but I shouldn't think she'd care.'

'What rules?'

'Screwing your client. Isn't it?' he asked, but not because he wanted an answer. 'Look – I can't simply ask you to leave now, but could you just lock up after you? You'll work it out,' he said.

He threw me a bunch of keys. Idiot boy.

'Sure,' I said nonchalantly. 'No problem.'

'I won't be back till tea – I promised Sophie we'd see *The Lion King*. Half-day today.'

'Right,' I said.

As if I care, I thought. I never want to see you again.

Did he leave with some idea that I was relieved, not saddened, by his departure?

When the front door slammed shut, I felt like a criminal. A secret agent. A spy. I would find her out. Each secret place would yield itself up to me like an opening shell. Let me catch her. Thief of my heart. Keeper of the Kingdom of the North.

I sat staring at her portrait for some time. What had Cliff said? That Howard painted just for a hobby? That he did 'something in the therapy world' too? Had all my instincts been accurate, then? He knew far more about therapy than I ever would. Dissembler.

There was something else Cliff had revealed about him. What

was it? I focused my mind. Of course! It slammed itself in my face like a prison door, locking me in with the two of them, together for ever, like Sartre's *Huis Clos*.

He had been Kate's client.

Kate's client! Not only mine, but Kate's. Kate's before he was mine, or was he Kate's still? So did she visit him in Chiswick, like a witch-doctor visits the sick, as I had seen her that day, to administer her secret therapy? Had he told her everything, just in the way that he was telling me, and did she love him now, because of it? Or in spite of it? Or both?

What was that noise?

I froze, petrified. Howard's warnings had taken root inside me. Kate was dangerous. I supposed it was just possible that she knew where I was. It was easy enough to guess. Did Howard know too? Had they followed me here together? Was I so obvious and unthinking in this cold twilight world of shadows and snow that my footprints ran away behind me like fickle messengers, reporting my path? Running from, not towards my goal?

I wanted to wash, but even my breath did not dare to move, let alone my body. I hated the feel of Cliff's juice swimming around inside. While I had undeniably complied with his seduction, Bill's 'rape' seemed as nothing now, by comparison. A hot contact of souls, no more. But this? In this contact, or complete lack of it, my soul had died of cold.

Another noise. This time I was sure that someone was there. Someone was on the stairs, creeping towards me. Very quietly.

I felt strangely calm. Almost confident. I waited like a wildcat, as if anticipating my prey, my equal, my match, whoever it was. It could only be Howard or Kate. Or possibly Rolf. Or Katherine's ghost? Whichever one it was, I knew their weaknesses now, all of them. I could fight and win. I reached for my bag and felt the small sharp knife nestling inside the pocket. Its blade felt hard and cold. I fingered the edge and the tip to reassure myself. Lethal, indeed.

The living-room door squeaked a little on its hinges, pushing open gently. I sat rigid. Silent. Alert. Nobody appeared. This move must be an invitation to investigate, one that was intended to catch me suddenly unawares. I had seen the movies. I knew what to do. Don't react. Wait. Be still.

At last I heard the timid miaow of BB, the Burmese cat, and found him at my feet, lashing his tail as he pressed himself against me. My relief was immense, revealing to me the true extent of my fear.

'Hello, Balthazar B! You terrifying animal!'

I picked him up and walked cautiously into the hall, his warm chocolate coat so comforting against my cheek. I stood there listening hard. BB was purring so loudly that any quiet sound would be hidden. I climbed the stairs, slowly and silently. I would make quite sure that I was alone now, that Kate was nowhere to be found, and then I would search the house for the essential clue that I had so foolishly lost. The locket.

As each room proved reassuringly empty, I began to breathe a little more easily. When finally I reached her bedroom – they had always had their separate rooms, Kate and Cliff, for reasons which were now quite clear – I exhaled the last remnants of anxiety.

'Right,' I said aloud, putting BB down again. 'Warn me if you find anything. If anyone comes in. Miaow at them like mad.'

I glanced around her bedroom, wondering whether her big brass bed had supported my husband's frame, or whether they tended to do it somewhere else, somewhere more neutral.

Or do they do it in my bed – our bed – at home, I wondered unwillingly. She would take pleasure in that.

I shuddered. I was in no doubt that she had taken pleasure in Howard up here. I could see them both vividly, like ghosts, their energies imprinting the atmosphere with their naked intensity.

I walked down a flight of stairs into her study, where she practised her therapy with a very select few. It was an airy, impersonal space. A stripped pine floor, lightly varnished. South-eastern sun. Almond-white walls. A colourful kilim rug in the middle of the room and another one on the wall, opposite a huge sash window with twelve panes of glass. Grand, sculptural plants – a palm, a yucca, the familiar swiss-cheese, its larger leaves leering over the desk as though reading each client's notes over Kate's shoulder as she scribbled them down. Two generous, comfortable sofas, face to face either side of the fireplace. Shelves full of books and files. Where was Howard's, then? Locked away somewhere?

I had intended to use the valuable time looking for the locket, but I found myself instead rifling through Kate's files, unashamedly at first, and then more furtively. At last Howard's name caught my eye.

North, H. Age 46. Occupation: Therapist/author.
Family history: Father left home after death of sister when H. aged 5. Brought up by mother. Incest.
Born: India. Nationality: British.
Aims and Objectives: To address problems with own sexuality.

I took a deep breath and sat down at her desk. I flicked through what I already knew, a file full of copious notes that

mirrored those I had made. Then suddenly a paragraph jumped
out at me:

> Expresses sexual interest in me. Aware of own attraction to
> client. Hard to separate. Objectivity? Difficult, if not imposs-
> ible. I ask what is his usual fantasy when sexually interested?
> 'To take off her clothes,' he says. I ask if she is active or
> passive in his fantasy? 'Passive,' he says. Is this fantasy
> designed to render his powerful mother impotent? (Re:
> incest.) Incapable of seducing him? I ask if she is at least
> conscious. 'Preferably not,' he says.

I stopped reading, momentarily. The memory of waking in
his Chiswick house, in nothing but a dressing-gown, floated
back to me. So he had taken advantage of me. Surely not raped
me? But certainly he had aroused himself while I was passive
to him, his favourite fantasy come true. I had somehow presumed that his arousal had been less calculated – a happy
coincidence, not a sought-for event. I read on, with some trepi-
dation now.

> I ask him if sexual interest in me is need to disempower
> me as the therapist/mother. He says, 'Fuck analysis. Don't
> interpret me,' which I read as yes.

Typical, I thought. Pig-arrogant.

> We talk about rules. H. hates them. Says, 'How can anyone
> treat sexual problems except sexually?' Feel excited. Turned
> on. Ask how he wants to be treated. He says he wants to
> learn healthy sexual exchange. Ask what's unhealthy for him
> currently? He says, 'I can't do it. I can only fuck Katherine.'

(His mother. Last had sex with her two months ago. She's now sixty-five). He refuses to see her now, indefinitely. Thinks distance from her will help solve problem. Finds distance v. difficult. Painful. Has he ever had sex with anyone else? 'No.' He is angry at my surprise. I reassure him. Aware I feel v. excited at thought of seducing client.

At least she's honest, I thought. But isn't this sad? And terrible? She can't seduce him. Where's the love in that? She would do the same thing to him all over again by seducing him.

I wanted to cradle Howard in my arms. Protect him. Shelter him from her storm.

A few pages later I found that he had taken off her clothes while she was fully conscious and that she had taken off his. This was seen as progress.

H. stands there with hard-on. He can't move. Standing two feet away from him. Aware I want him. Losing objectivity. Ask him what he wants. 'I want to fuck you,' he says. Not make love. Fuck. Feel doubly turned on. His body is beautiful. I invite him to. I roll a condom over his dick. He pulls it off. Goes soft. 'I can't do it,' he says. Gets dressed. I'm still naked. I tell him I want him. He freaks. 'Where's your professionalism?' he asks. I get dressed. When he's gone, I have to masturbate.

I looked out at the garden, full of their children's toys and swings. Do they play doctors-and-nurses out there, while she plays it in here?

How pathetically reduced in meaning the sexual act seemed to me then. I wondered if I would ever be able to make love again. Or whether I would only have sex, just as I had done that morning with Cliff, in some half-gratifying, half-horrifying rape of the soul. Clandestine squalor.

I read on. There was a great deal more of the same. During almost every session they would try to have reciprocal sex. During one session they both masturbated themselves after a failed attempt to masturbate each other. Howard still couldn't achieve orgasm. On and on it went, almost every week for a year. By the time they started looking for Howard's mother, in the hope that he might be able to resolve his problem by talking it through with her, Kate sounded unimaginably frustrated, beyond what she could comfortably endure. She was obsessed with Howard. She lived in desperate hope of a physical consummation of this obsession, which seemed no longer to regard his needs at all.

I heard BB the cat miaow loudly outside the door. My blood ran cold. What if she was there right now? Waiting? I was trapped. I didn't even have my knife.

I crept to the shelf and replaced Howard's file. Then I stood behind the door, opening it slowly. BB trotted in, rubbing himself against my legs and then against the legs of the desk, purring loudly. I peered through the crack at the hinge-end of the door, but I couldn't see anyone. I waited for BB to venture out again. I figured that he would also rub himself against anyone else's legs the other side of the door. When he did eventually leave the room, however, he simply trotted upstairs towards the bedrooms.

I followed him, snatching the very blunt paper-knife from Kate's desk, as well as a heavy piece of petrified wood that served as a paperweight. I hoped that this could knock a person out without really hurting them.

Again I approached each door with the same absurd terror

that had accompanied my first search through the house, an hour earlier. And again I finished up in Kate's bedroom. It was surely the room most likely to hide the lost clue from view. I intended to search every inch of it.

I put my weapons on the bed where I could easily reach them. Then I shut the door, placing BB outside on the landing, as a sort of lookout. Although such precautions seemed excessive, even neurotic, to me, I felt safer for them. They enabled me to concentrate on the task at hand, which proved increasingly difficult, the less I was able to find.

I began with the obvious places – drawers, boxes, shelves. I even pulled the drawers out altogether to see if anything was taped on to their ends, or hidden behind them. Floorboards came up (the loose ones, at least), pillows and mattresses were examined for recent stitching, I went through the pockets of all her remaining clothes, I checked the ceiling light, the wall-lights, the architrave around the door, the architrave around the windows, the frames of paintings and prints, I checked everything. Short of using a trained sniffer-dog, I couldn't have been more thorough in my search.

But I didn't find the locket. What I did find was very interesting to me, but of no use to North.

I found a book by Neville Hoare, hidden in the mattress. She had cut the outer fabric at the corner seam, and had slipped the book through. Then she had stitched the fabric loosely at the end. The book was his most recent and radical, one that I still hadn't finished reading, called *Beyond the Law*. The subtitle ran: 'Why the individual conscience seeks revenge for a crime which the law fails to recognize as crime.' The word 'revenge' lashed out at me like a brandished knife.

Kate wants revenge, I told myself. That's the exact word he used.

The book was inscribed: 'The law punishes those whom it fails to protect. We must protect those whom it fails to punish. Your secret is safe with me, as mine is with you.' It was signed 'H.N. or N.H. – choose.'

Cryptic though the message was, one thing was certain. Howard North and Neville Hoare were one and the same. The clues had been there all along. But I had missed every one of them.

My heart jumped with a strange kind of joy. I had met him, after all! I had met Neville Hoare! He had turned to me for help!

I sat on the bed with the book in my hand, beaming like an infatuated teenager. I had felt something similar at fifteen, when a lead singer had smiled at me during one of his gigs.

But before I could really grasp the full wonder of my discovery, it happened – far too fast.

I heard a key in the front door. I heard it open, pause, then close. I heard footsteps – a woman's – crisp and firm in the hall. I heard them climb the stairs, fearless steps up flight after flight towards me, pausing only on the floor below to open and close her study door. Then in no time at all I could hear her coming for me. Up the final flight. I could even hear her breath. Everything in the bedroom was upside-down, and she was coming for me. I knew it was Kate. And she knew it was me. Even if she'd had any doubt, my yellow Mini would have convinced her that I was already there, already searching. I only just had time to grab the paperweight before she opened the door.

'I thought I'd find you here.'

She stood quite still, rigid with rage, as her eyes took in the thoroughness of my search.

'Did you find what you were looking for?' she asked, her

face as hard as stone, her mouth a thin line drawn an inch across.

The book was lying beside me, title up.

I couldn't say anything. My mouth was too dry. I held the petrified wood in my fist, my hand hidden under her bedcover. She walked towards me and picked up the book.

'Was this what you were looking for?' she asked, a slight sneer creasing her mouth.

I shook my head.

She must see how terrified I am, I thought. I'm defenceless. She's caught me at my weakest, most open moment of all.

'What do you make of the inscription?' she asked quizzically.

'I don't,' I rasped back.

'Mystifying, isn't it?'

'Quite,' I agreed.

Above all, I wanted her to think me completely ignorant of everything I suspected or knew. I had plenty of my own ideas about what the inscription meant, but I wasn't going to be drawn by her.

'H.N. or N.H. Whose initials are those?'

'Neville Hoare's, I suppose,' I answered pathetically.

'Aren't you clever?' she said, like a sweet mother to a child.

I smiled a feeble smile.

'But not quite as half-intelligent as I know you are,' she jabbed. 'What about H.N.? Whose initials are those?'

'Howard's?' I volunteered.

'Clever girl!' she patronized. 'Very good indeed, Little Molly Brown.'

My childhood nicknames jeered back at me over the years. Little Molly Brown. Scrawny Brawny Brown. Good Golly Miss Molly. Molly Golly Gosh.

'Did he tell you already?'

'What?'

'About being Neville Hoare?'

I shook my head.

'Don't sit there shaking your head like an ornamental dog. If you mean no, say no, slag.'

'No.'

'Why should I believe you?'

'Because it's true.'

'What else is true?' she asked.

That was when she took out the gun. A small revolver, gleaming like a toy.

'What else is true?' she asked again, pointing the gun at me.

'What are you doing?' I yelped. 'Kate!'

'Just like a dog, aren't you? Sniffing around for bones.'

I felt the cold metal nudge my head.

'Talk,' she said.

'Wh— what about?'

'Aren't you cowardly?' She almost laughed. 'I had no idea what a coward you were! All those fights, eh? Scrawny Brawny Brown! I could've slayed you every time! Couldn't I?' she asked, pressing the gun into my temple until it throbbed there.

'Yes,' I acquiesced meekly.

'You're a coward, Mo. Not Howard's type at all. He admires strength, I'm afraid. Fallen for him, haven't you? But he's in love with me. Idiot.'

'I'm not in – I haven't –'

'He laughs at you,' she sneered, cutting me off. 'We laugh at you together, Mo. And Bill does too. We all laugh at you.'

Her spite was nothing new. As a small girl she had wielded extraordinary power with her sharp, evil tongue, her sadistic lies cutting into people's hearts. She was remorseless. I had forgotten this side of Kate, had perhaps even imagined that she had outgrown it, but I wasn't surprised when it reappeared. My worst fears resurfaced, like fleeting visitors.

'Unfortunately, however,' she resumed, satisfied that she had caused me pain, 'I can't return his love. Not any more.'

She paused.

'Aren't you curious?' she asked. 'Don't you long to know why?'

'I suppose so,' I said.

'I'll tell you anyway. Whether you like it or not. He's a murderer. That's why. He killed his own mother, you see. Did he tell you that?' She didn't expect a reply. 'Now I don't think that's nice. I really don't like that sort of behaviour in a man. D'you know what I mean?'

'Mmm,' I mumbled.

'Sorry? Didn't hear you?'

She lifted my chin with the gun so that I was looking at her. She smiled adorably, like her portrait, an angelic Botticelli face radiating love and even compassion for me.

'I said mmm. I do know what you mean.'

'Good. That's good. Little Molly Brown. I'm glad you know what I mean. I don't feel so alone now.'

She dropped my chin again, withdrawing the gun. She crossed her arms, the gun now pointing at some random target in the direction of one of the windows.

If I jump at her now, I thought, and hit her with the paperweight, the gun will go off over there. It'll hit the window. Someone outside will see the glass break and call the police.

I almost did this, thinking that, with surprise on my side, I was bound to triumph over her, but then I wondered how many bullets were loaded in her gun. I realized that she was unlikely to drop it, and that a second bullet might easily lodge itself somewhere inside me. She'd call it self-defence.

'I wouldn't try anything, Mo.'

'Neither would I,' I said.

She paused indolently.

'Some people like that in a man. That kind of violence. They think it means he's rough – dominant in bed. Women like that, don't they?' She studied my face for a response. 'Don't they, Mo?'

'Do they?' I mumbled sheepishly, thinking of Cliff.

'Whereas, funnily enough, he's very gentle in bed. When eventually you get him there. He likes to be taken. He likes to be seduced.'

'Right,' I said.

'What d'you mean, right? You know this already, do you?'

'No,' I said. 'I'm just – listening.'

'Envious? I liked seducing him. Oh, I seduced him in the end all right. I wonder if that's what tipped the balance for him. He had to kill her then.'

There was some plausibility in this wild theory of hers. It made too much sense now, after what I'd read in her notes. I began to suspect him all over again, in spite of myself. I thought of him standing naked and frustrated in her room. I thought of his need for my objectivity. And hers. His insistence that I did not fall in love with him. Why? Because of what happened when Kate had fallen for him?

It all adds up, I thought. Kate is just a woman scorned, no more dangerous than that. Though that's dangerous enough. He's the killer. Not her. He sees her as dangerous because he can't face the danger in himself. He puts it outside him still, even a clever man like Neville Hoare. Even he projects his violence on to others.

'What are you thinking about?' she demanded.

'I was thinking you were possibly right.'

'About what?'

'About murdering his mother – the reasons –'

'Of course I'm right! It has to be that.'

Her face showed sudden pain. I seized my opportunity.

'You look very sad, Kate.'

Tears filled her eyes and spilled over.

'He's let me down,' she moaned like a wounded animal.

'Sure,' I agreed sympathetically. Possibly he had.

'How dare you pity me!' she bellowed, her mood switching direction like a sweeping punch, impossible to anticipate or avoid.

The gun was at my temple again, this time pressed against it hard. I felt I was suspended from it, a dangling, trembling puppet waiting for her to pull. Or would she release the strings entirely, letting me crumple down as if she had set me free? A sweet act of love, like euthanasia? I stopped breathing. My bowels lurched into spasms of uncontrollable fear.

'I – I need the loo,' I said absurdly.

She sneered at me, my terror pleasuring her like a favourite comedy.

'It's you who's pitiful, Mo!' She laughed mercilessly. 'It's you we're all laughing at, dear!'

She shoved her face in mine. Her chocolate-brown eyes, which always promised heavenly tastes, seemed murky as sewers close up. Did mine too?

'What have you ever done with your miserable, pathetic little life? What tiny thing have you ever achieved? You can't work, you can't breed, you can't cook, you can't even pay your own bills! It's no wonder he's left you, is it? You can't even satisfy your own husband, Mo!'

She'd relinquished the sweeping-punch technique to plunge the knife in, twisting it like a screw, turning it inside me like a torturer.

A host of retaliatory jibes tickled my tongue. I bit my bottom lip so that I could not utter a word. Any word that left me then would have sentenced me to death.

'He's a fabulous lover, I have to admit,' she said.

Pause.

She was waiting. I wanted to scream.

Swap our positions, I thought, and I'd pull the trigger now.

'The best I've ever known. Better than Howard. Just. Easily better than Cliff.' She smiled whimsically.

I swapped lips, biting the top one now. I could taste the blood on my teeth. Waves of nausea washed over me.

I hate her, I thought. I hate her now.

'But you've not had many to compare him with, have you? You didn't know how lucky you were. Poor diddums. Too late now.'

I had the terrible thought that she had done something violent to him.

'Where is he?' I blurted out.

'You mean you care?' she asked in mock-surprise.

'What have you done to him?'

'Oh, dear,' she said ominously. 'What have I done?'

Please be alive, Bill. Please.

'Tell me what you've done,' I said.

'Dear, oh dear, oh me . . .'

I clenched the paperweight. The petrified wood.

'We thought we were getting over you,' she said, explaining her 'mistake' to me. 'We didn't know you cared.'

'We.' How I loathed 'we'.

'What does that mean?'

But she didn't reply. She stared wistfully into the middle distance, like someone with a conscience.

'What does that *mean*, Kate?' I insisted.

My voice betrayed my dread.

She played on this, shaking her head tragically.

'Didn't he – surely he left you a note?' she asked dramatically.

She was the picture of concern, as if wondering, aghast, whether her well-meaning attempt to nurse Bill through what they assumed was my adultery had been a mistake; did I want him, after all?

This isn't my world, I thought. Take me back to the gentle climate I trusted as a child. I never wanted this.

'If he's still alive –' she said – 'and we did discuss the option of suicide quite thoroughly – but if he is still alive, he'll be exploring other women, I hope. We thought that was the obvious route for him – after me.'

I stared at her dumbly, stupefied.

'Are you mad?' I asked.

'You're only a beginner, Mo. You'll learn. You're a scrawny, old-fashioned stick-in-the-mud. All your little prejudices about sex . . .'

'I don't have prejudices, Kate. I have a belief-system.'

'Oh, that,' she said drily. 'I used to have one of those!'

What a world of difference there is, I thought, between Kate's therapy and Steph's. The-Rapist or the therapist. Didn't Bill see that?

'I have a code of ethics, Kate. I wouldn't be without one.'

But even as the words left my bitten lips, I thought of my morning with Cliff. What ethics there? To use another woman's husband, a willing accomplice, admittedly, but a man with whom I could not have, and did not want, any further intimacy. A body, no more. One who had stood in ingloriously, like an understudy in a play, without the slightest chance of any further success. A man incapable of embodying any of the charisma, intelligence or depth that made the true man so irresistible. I had used him, eyes closed, as a poor substitute for the real thing, at a desperate moment.

'That's what he likes about you, isn't it?' she said plainly.

'What?' I asked, shamefaced.

'Your ethical code, you dumb whore. Isn't it?'

'I don't understand.'

'That's what our killer likes about you!' she shouted furiously, enviously, in my face. 'He likes your ethical pontifications, I should think. Your opinionated moral judgements, your anally-retentive moral-high-ground pious high-and-mighty thou-shalt-nots.'

She stared at me triumphantly, as if she had found me out at last. As if I had been dealing in a false currency behind her back. As if I had cheated her of her only prize by some mean, dirty, low-down trick. As if at last she had found a weapon against me, a lie that she could tell, something to dishonour me. In fact, if what she said was true, I had simply played a trump card that she didn't have – a sense of right and wrong, albeit my own – that she would never have now. She had thrown hers away, many years ago. Was I also losing touch with mine? Unbeknownst to myself?

'I always think of Neville Hoare as someone who would deplore anyone with the characteristics you've just described.'

'I'm not talking about Neville bloody Hoare. Who said I was talking about Hoare?'

'Our killer, you said.'

'North's the killer. North's our man. Hoare doesn't exist. All that great liberating crap about the human mind! It's all written by a fictional character! Imagine if they knew! I long for them to know. The greatest, most innovative thinker of our time since Foucault or Freud! And who is he? Fiction-head. Fantasy-brain. Fuck-wit non-existent pervert who can't have sex! Recovering

Catholic boy who for his whole life has wanted to run along the moral tramlines of the Catholic Church. While he was having sex with his own mother! His own bloody mother! Did he tell you that?'

I didn't answer.

'I bet he didn't tell you that, did he? He saves that for the women who can't cope with it.'

'Does he?'

'The women who remind him of her. The possessive ones.'

How she revealed herself at every turn!

'Or should I say the obsessive ones? The ones who've managed perfectly well without needing men, without needing more than the occasional servicing from men. The beautiful ones, who can pick and choose. Those women who aren't afraid to challenge him, who don't just bend over backwards for his body and brains. They're the ones he tells. The ones he can destroy.'

She said this as if the fact that she had been told North's great secret somehow reflected a superiority in her.

'Whereas you, Scrawny Brawny Brown, you don't tax his brain for more than a minute or two. I happen to know that. He likes your simplicity. Your moral straightforwardness. Your naïve view of the world. But you bore him rigid, Mo. Sorry about that. He's just using you. Thinks it'll spice up our sex life somewhat if I get a little jealous of you.'

Her eyes ran over me searchingly, almost with a perverse kind of desire.

'Frankly, he's wrong. Now if he'd chosen someone even half-interesting, even half-enigmatic, with a tiny percentage of real sex-appeal, then possibly, yes, I might've been a little jealous of her. But you? Jealous of you! Well it's silly, isn't it? How could I ever be jealous of someone like you?'

225

She *was* jealous. There was no doubt about it. Howard had withdrawn his attentions from her and had focused them on me. She hadn't got her own way. She'd lost him. She hadn't conquered him. But she thought I had.

Had I, I asked myself in astonishment. Perhaps I had.

The possibility ran like an electric current through me, excited me, thrilled me. Howard North. Neville Hoare. I even dared myself to think of a future with him. A vibrant, challenging life with a man I truly admired. Admired and desired. Who would need children then?

I thought of Bill, of our ten wretched years of trying to have children, as though nothing else could have made the marriage meaningful. And yet he was a part of me, and I a part of him. We had grown together like two entwined plants. I wondered if our separation would kill us both outright? Even though what we shared was only history. The sudden possibility of really leaving him, not just of losing him defeatedly in exchange for loneliness, but of leaving him behind in exchange for a better love, better life, seemed brutal and shocking, as never before.

'Or is it some part of your body?' she asked suddenly. 'Some secret part of you hidden away in there that I can't see?'

'Sorry?'

'No! It can't be! I've seen your miserable little body often enough,' she sneered. 'There's nothing worth having there.'

Her gun prodded at my chest.

'If I were a man, I'd rape you now,' she said.

'That's nice,' I replied.

'Maybe it's the way you screw.'

She paused. I sensed that she was wondering how she could rape me, how she could somehow experience my love-making.

'What does he want from you?' she screamed, her face red

with rage, up against mine. 'What does he want from a barren, sterile hag like you?'

She tore my shirt open and grabbed at my breasts, fresh from her husband's earlier assault. A feeling of revulsion surged through me.

'What are you doing?'

'These! Is it these?' she half-laughed, half-wailed. 'Is it these feeble attempts at fulsomeness he wants? These dry, milkless founts!'

She slapped my breasts contemptuously, degradingly, then pulled at them as if they were dugs – udders to be milked dry . . .

'Get off me,' I said coldly, fingering the heavy wood in my hand.

She stuck the gun in my mouth.

'Or is it that you give good head? Is it because you've got nothing else to offer him, you have to suck him off instead? Like some cheap whore?'

One slight move now and she would pull the trigger. I was sure of it. We were both edging out of control. She needed my fear again, my meek subservience. She had always loved power.

Give it to her, I thought. Pacify her. Let her think she has control of me.

I closed my eyes, the gun deep in my mouth.

If she thrusts it any further down my throat, I'll retch, I thought.

'I'll have to kill you anyway now,' she said nonchalantly.

I didn't believe her but I looked at her pleadingly, none the less.

'Well, I've told you Howard's secret now, haven't I? And that's unethical.'

I tried to speak through the gun. She withdrew it from my mouth.

'What?' she ordered. 'What did you say?'

'He'd told me already,' I said.

'Told you what?'

'His secret.'

'Which one?' A brief pause. 'Answer the question, you disgusting hag.'

'The secret about his mother. And him.'

She looked at me in disbelief.

'*You?* She seemed almost revolted. 'He told *you*?'

I nodded meekly.

'I hate you,' she said, lifting her gun to my head.

She said it in a way that I believed. A matter-of-fact way. Her finger moved on the trigger. I hit the gun from her hand but it didn't fall. It shot the mattress. Her arm moved again, as if for a second aim. I took her wrist with one hand so that I could control her aim. With my other hand, while she scrambled to break free of my grip, I hit her with the petrified wood. She dropped the gun and shielded her head with both hands. She was suddenly unsteady on her feet. There was blood running slowly through her fingers. She stumbled backwards, her head cracking on the wall as she fell against it. She slid down the wall until she was sort of crouching. She moaned with the pain. I picked up the gun.

'Kate?'

She moaned again. I wanted to see the wound, to see that it was real, serious, deep, before I would help her. I feared that she was deceiving me, that she would wait until I was close to her, then grab the gun and shoot.

'Let me see,' I said, pointing the gun at her. 'Take your hands away from your head.'

She ignored me.

'For God's sake!' I shouted, panicking now.

She moaned again.

'Are you all right?' I asked urgently. 'Shall I call an ambulance?'

She didn't respond. Instead she took her hands away from her head to look at the blood.

'I'll call an ambulance,' I said, as soon as I saw.

We waited in silence, in limbo, like two astronauts floating in space. I felt helpless. Powerless. Lost in shock.

How do I explain? I wondered. The room looked like the aftermath of a burglary. They will ask us what happened. What will she say? And who will they believe? Who would I believe?

I wiped the gun with the bedcover, regretting that I'd picked it up. If only her fingerprints alone had been all over it, I could have argued a case. But now? What evidence did I have now? I knew she would frame me somehow. Just as she was trying to frame North. This TV personality's word against mine? And in her own home?

When the ambulance arrived, I let the crew in. She explained that I had threatened to kill her. That's how it happened. I was a murderer.

'Would I call you,' I said, 'if I wanted her dead?'

They said that I'd better accompany her. I thought so too.

After various examinations, they helped her to her feet. I followed behind, my tail between my legs like a dog.

Kate was still wearing her coat, I noticed, although it was a little bloody by then. It wasn't a coat I'd seen her wear before. It was an elegant coat. Well-cut. I thought I'd seen it somewhere before, on somebody else.

I probably have, I told myself. What does it matter?

But it troubled me. I knew it was significant, somehow.

'You'll have to ride in front, love,' somebody said to me.

It was only when we passed a couple of drunks, staggering down the middle of the road, that I remembered. I remembered the tramp in Bloomsbury. And I remembered the coat, sweeping past me towards her as if to help, and then sweeping on. Leaving her bloody and dead. Kate's coat.

Who would believe me now?

23

She was soon unconscious, thankfully. I was safe from her lies until she came round again. Assuming that she would.

Would she? I wondered. Suppose she dies?

A wild panic seized me.

Suppose I've killed her? I thought.

I followed the stretcher as they wheeled her past reception, turning left through swing-doors, half-way down a corridor that seemed to have no end, which seemed to beckon me on and on down its shiny, slippery surface of blue.

'Would you mind waiting outside, madam?' a male nurse ordered me.

'Of course.' I paused. 'Not,' I corrected myself: 'Of course not. Do I have to make a statement or anything?'

'Do you?' he replied.

'It was an accident,' I said.

'If you need to make a statement, madam, you'd better telephone the police. I'll ask reception. They'll do it for you.'

What had I said?

'I don't think I do,' I said.

'Perhaps someone has called them already?' he asked.

'Not to my knowledge,' I said.

'None of the ambulance crew?'

'Not to my knowledge,' I said. But perhaps they had.

'You'd better wait in reception, madam,' he said coldly, reaching for the telephone.

I waited in reception obediently. It was only a very short time before two policemen came in and made an inquiry at the desk, while a car flashed its blue lights outside. I couldn't hear what they said, but they were directed down the same long corridor and turned off through the same swing-doors.

Then Howard came in. He walked directly towards me and sat down at my side. He hardly moved his lips.

'I'll follow you,' he whispered. 'Just walk out very calmly. Turn left. Wait by the car, as inconspicuously as possible. I'll be right behind you.'

I obeyed, without any hesitation. I trusted him, I realized, implicitly.

He drove very fast, down back roads I'd never seen, until we were careering along the M1 motorway, due north.

'Where are we going?' I asked, finally.

'Scotland. It's rather an obvious route. But it's the fastest. I'm counting on their inefficiency.'

'Why Scotland?'

'It's a good place to hide.'

'How do you know?'

'I don't. I'm guessing.

Pause.

'Is this really the right thing to do?' I asked.

'Are you serious?'

'It looks so suspicious, doesn't it?'

'I'll tell you what looks suspicious,' he barked. 'You going in there. Cliff coming out. You staying in. Kate going in. Kate coming out dripping with blood, carried off in an ambulance. You following. Witnesses galore.'

I let this sequence of images sink in.

'I take it you followed me after all. Despite what I'd said?'

I demanded crossly, ashamed of anything else he might have seen.

'What were you going to do? Give yourself up? Expect justice?' he asked in disbelief.

'Watch your speed,' I said, seeing a police car ahead.

He dropped back abruptly, into the middle lane.

The day felt unreal. Something to wake up from. A movie. A book. A dream. Something that should end, leaving me thankful for my mediocre life.

'They'll call it attempted murder, Mo.' He issued the statement like a kindly lawyer, trying to persuade himself of my innocence.

'It wasn't,' I said, 'attempted murder.'

'What was it, then?'

'Self-defence.'

'Was it the gun she threatened you with? I thought I heard a shot.'

'What do you mean, was it the gun?'

'She threatened the old boy with a gun and a knife.'

I thought of the knife in my bag, still sitting on the sofa of Kate's living-room. How would that look to anyone investigating the case?

'Yes. It was the gun. She was about to pull the trigger. That's the only reason I –'

'Did you touch the gun?'

'Yes, I did.'

'Higgs . . .' He sighed, shaking his head.

'I wiped it afterwards.'

'Worse still. Everything points to you. She's not stupid, Mo.'

'But she's mad! You should've heard some of the things she was saying!'

'Do you think they'd believe you?'

'It's the truth,' I said, simply.

But no. I didn't think they'd believe me. And the terror of not being believed shot through me like a bullet.

'Bill will believe me, won't he?'

'Will he?' Howard asked, unconvinced. 'Wasn't he having an affair with her? While you were off playing with a suspected murderer?'

'But he's my husband.'

I was aware of the ridiculousness of this statement, and yet it felt like such a good reason for his trust.

Is there no such thing as justice, after all, I asked myself. At best, I should be cosseted now, counselled out of my shock, protected, reassured. At worst, I should be released after various court hearings, while Kate should receive two life sentences. For attempted murder and murder itself.

'What did your mother look like when she died?' I asked. 'Was she – poor?'

'My mother?' He glanced at me in surprise, before his eyes returned to the road ahead. 'She looked like a – like wax.'

'I mean, what was she wearing, what was her hair like, what –'

'Yes, she was poor,' he said. 'She looked like someone who had lived on the streets for two years.' He sounded sorry, as if it were his fault.

'Had she?'

'In all likelihood. Her fellow cardboard-box dwellers said she'd been looking for me. She came to London for the day and never went back.'

'So she looked – what? Like a tramp?'

'I suppose you might say that,' he conceded. 'She looked like Katherine to me. Only she was dead. And her eyes had gone. She was blind.'

Everything fell into place.

'You didn't kill her, did you?' It was more of a statement than a question.

'You tell me,' he said.

'I know you didn't.'

He smiled. A smile of relief? That someone else believed him at last?

'I think I know how you must have felt, all this time,' I said.

'You'll know soon,' he confirmed.

I saw the days ahead, the knowing days. They stretched before me like the long, beckoning hospital corridor, unremittingly bleak.

'Kate killed her, didn't she?' I said, out of the blue.

He shrugged.

'Didn't she?' I wanted her crime admitted, at least. I knew that he knew.

He wouldn't answer me. I thought of his inscription in Kate's book. That 'secret' of hers, 'safe' with him. Why wouldn't he tell me the truth?

'Why didn't Katherine just – just go to your house? She must have known where you lived?' I asked.

'Nobody knew. I'd only recently moved.'

'But surely you –'

'Surely what?' he snapped, cutting me off.

'I suppose that, being Neville Hoare, you –'

'Who told you that?' he snapped again, the car swerving slightly.

'I guessed. I found a book of Kate's,' I admitted. 'The initials –'

'I see,' he said coldly.

We both fell silent, estranged. We drove on for another half-hour without saying a word.

Finally he spoke.

'She didn't have my address because – because I was trying to break free of her. And Kate had suggested that I spend less time with her. Or in fact no time with her. But I failed to explain to her why. I just – I just stopped visiting. After forty-six years of being there almost all the time.' He paused. 'It must have been very painful for her.'

Somehow I didn't care very much any more about Howard's woes. I had too many of my own. If I could have done anything then to turn back the clock, to have my chance again, I would have done it. I would have loved my ordinary, mediocre, unsuccessful life more than anything. I would have loved to eat and sleep and garden and shop and be lonely and row.

'You remember our first session?' he said, pulling me back to the present.

'How could I forget it?' I said.

'Do you remember my face had been slightly rearranged?'

'Yes. You were very stubborn about not telling me why.'

'I hit Kate.'

Of course. Her swollen cheek. So he was responsible for that. It was all tied in together, just I had suspected. But so what? It was too late now.

'I hit her because I thought she'd killed my mother. And she, being Kate, fearless and feminist, hit me back.'

'I see,' I said, no longer interested, since there was nothing I could do about it now. There was nothing I could do about anything now.

'I picked up your passport, by the way,' he said. 'You might need it.'

'My passport?'

'I'm afraid I had to break in through your french doors.'

'Why?' I asked stupidly.

'To get it.'

'When?'

'When I saw the ambulance. And Kate. I thought it would be sensible.'

'You're like a minder,' I said.

I didn't want to be with him, I realized. I blamed him. I felt that he had lured me away from my dead life into a fatal trap. And now I couldn't escape. My freedom was gone. *My freedom.*

'Will I see Bill again?'

'Do you want to?'

'Of course I do.'

'Then you will.'

'How will he know where I am?'

'I'll tell him.'

'Promise me,' I said desperately.

'I promise you,' he said kindly, hearing the wretchedness in my voice. A wretchedness that he knew only too well. The great big loss of love.

We stayed the night in a remote hotel. Or perhaps it was a bed and breakfast – I didn't know. I did know that it was miles from anywhere. We checked in as Mr and Mrs Andrews and I dreamt of Gainsborough's painting all night long.

The beds stood four feet apart. We slept fully dressed. I felt no fear. I didn't know whether this was because I felt safe, or whether it was just that I didn't care any more.

In the morning Howard brought a large breakfast up to the room for me. He refused a hot, buttered bread roll.

'I've eaten,' he said.

He stood at the window, staring out over the snow on the moors.

'It's a beautiful view,' I said.

'Yes,' he agreed dreamily, then added more resolutely, 'I'm going for a drive – see if I can find somewhere.'

'Find somewhere?'

'To stay. Keep a low profile, won't you? News is already out.'

When he went, I wondered if he'd ever come back. Probably not, I thought. Too dangerous.

I sat on the window-seat of our heavy-panelled room and gazed at the snow all day. The bleak relentlessness of the rolling moors seemed to insist on a warm inner life, since no comfort could be had without; the climate seemed to reject my frail humanity. God help me, I thought. What warmth can I hope to find inside me now?

I remembered the dream I had, that last night of love with Bill. The unbearable cold. The rules I didn't understand. The punishing.

What had I done?

I was asleep when Howard returned, my head against the window like a dog waiting stubbornly for a walk.

'Any joy?' I asked, feeling a little joy myself on seeing him again.

'Possibly,' he said.

He was uncommunicative. He kept his head bowed low, as though weighed down by too much thought. Worry. Gravitas.

'Anything I can do?'

'Cut your hair. Sound Scottish. Change,' he said. 'Be someone else.'

We stayed in the same hotel for another two nights. I didn't leave our room once. I didn't dare. Not for anything.

Howard helped me to cut my hair, holding mirrors at difficult angles so that I could see. By the time we'd finished, I looked like a boy. An urchin. The mousey-brown tufts stood away from my narrow face in shock.

We practised my Scottish dialect whenever we spoke. I was forbidden the use of my native tongue. Howard was as pedantic as Higgins in Shaw's *Pygmalion*. We created a history and an occupation for me, a new name, an introverted personality, a way of walking, of dressing, of writing, of everything. A whole new identity. Howard even bought me a pair of spectacles, which I found too obvious by far, but with which he was so delighted that I finally acquiesced. They were a dark tortoise-shell which made me look very stern, and they were very round. The overall effect was of a thin, startled, rather angry owl.

We laughed at me a lot. The laughter of the lost. Partners in crime.

'Why are you doing this for me?'

'Scottish!' he ordered.

'Why are yer doing this fer mee?' I asked Scottishly.

'Doowin' . . .' he corrected.

'Why are yer doowin' this fer mee?'

'Nay bad, lass! Nay bad at all!' he exclaimed triumphantly.

But he didn't answer the question. On reflection I realized that his reasons were self-evident. He was a man obsessed with ideals. Ideologies. His own set of rules. His truth, which denied accepted morality. And his truth, or story, spilled into mine. In protecting me from the judgement of others, he was protecting himself. He was a man who stood outside the law. He was Neville Hoare.

We left in the early hours of the third morning so that no one would see us. Or me. Howard wouldn't tell me what news was out, whether my photograph had been printed anywhere, or even whether anyone knew that he was on the run with me. Instead he simply cultivated in me an immense enthusiasm for my role as Urchin-Wonder of the North. So that I'd convince, fearlessly.

I was conscious that I was surrendering my will entirely to his direction, but I had no other choice. Without his faith in me, his humour and kindness and love, I'd have surrendered to the law at once. I lacked his strength.

Our next stop was a monastery on the Isle of Iona. A haven of gentleness. A place to die.

We took a boat via the Isle of Mull and earned our keep at the monastery by occasional labours of love. Ordinary, pleasurable chores like cooking, cleaning, tilling the soil, pruning fruit-trees, fixing a leaking roof, clearing paths through the snow. Summer would be the busy time there, when crops were tended and harvested for food.

I would have stayed there a lifetime, sheltering from the blizzard that roared through my days, but Howard allowed us a fortnight and no more.

'They'll start asking questions soon.'

'We can answer them,' I said.

'How? With lies?' He respected the truth in curious ways. 'We must seem like innocent civilians, just enjoying a fortnight's retreat.'

We left the following day, back on the boat, eating smoked mussels with plastic forks from polystyrene trays.

Loch Tay was our destination. I was reading the map. A cottage was vacant there which Howard had rented for me. The contracts had been exchanged, unbeknownst to me, two days previously. Howard had arranged for us to have access before all the paperwork was done. We drove via Perth to pick up the keys.

'How much is it?' I asked, bewildered by gratitude.

'Very little. It's only very basic, Mo.'

And although it was 'only very basic', the view was breath-taking. The two front rooms of the cottage, both the bedroom and living-room, looked straight out over the water – an enormous expanse of fresh, deep blue that harboured the blowing sails of boats – yellows, reds, whites, greens – surrounded by mountainous slopes of woodland and grass.

I opened the window and breathed in the air.

'It smells of the sea!' I said joyfully.

Howard grinned, indulging my childish glee.

'The garden has a couple of fruit-trees, an apple and a pear, I think, which doubtless need pruning soon –'

'Lovely,' I said.

'Then there's a clematis, a honeysuckle, and countless roses, I'm afraid. Can't abide them, myself.'

I thought of the garden at his mother's house.

'Too much of a good thing . . .' I said.

'Possibly,' he agreed. He seemed glad of my intuitive response.

We were caught suddenly in a startling web of desire, like two unsuspecting flies.

He reached out a hand. I took it willingly. He drew me towards him, wrapping his arms around me like two big angel's wings. He breathed in my aroma and sighed, as once he had breathed in Richmond Park's heavenly scent. He kissed me tentatively, like a shy boy, stroking my short tufts of hair with his big warm hand. Then he stood away from me a little, holding me at arm's length, smiling peacefully.

'I knew I was right about you,' he said, but wouldn't explain what he meant.

Instead he set about lighting the fire, while I explored the territory, standing a good ten minutes in each particular space: the two bedrooms, the kitchen, the bathroom, and finally the garden, rolling down the hill towards Loch Tay.

Perhaps I've died, I thought, and this is my afterlife.

In the evening we cooked some potatoes from the monastery, and ate them with a jar of mayonnaise and a packet of cold ham. Then we opened a cheap bottle of wine, sitting by the fire, close as lovers might be.

'I'll have to leave you tomorrow,' he said. 'First thing. Before they start looking for my car.'

Don't go, I thought. This is my paradise and you are my angel, my Gabriel, guardian Gabriel angel, who carries me on wings away from birds of prey.

We lay naked under our coats by the fire on the floor and caressed our longing limbs. I slept, and dreamt of *The Water Babies*. When I woke we were at love, in love, in the middle of love, in the making of the middle of love. Sweet love, like penetrating songs, like an angel's high notes or like the pealing of bells through our surrendering cells. Then we slept, then loved again, and so on in the same sweet way until the break of day.

Who am I now, I wondered. Nobody I know.

Stripped of the fabric of my life, those threads that wove a place for me in other people's days, I felt free. Just when I thought that freedom was gone, that my life was dead, I felt more alive and free than ever before. The cluttering constraints of my old reality were shed from me as easily as clothes. I was free of guilt, free of grief, free of duty and show.

Blessed. Free to begin again. Resurrected in love.

24

In the morning a memory came back to me very clearly. Had it returned in an effort to make sense of things? I remembered the day we got the news about the shooting.

Bill was in South Africa. We'd only been married two months. At the door there were two police officers, in uniform. They made me go over to Kate's, where Cliff could look after us, before they would say anything. Kate wasn't famous then. She made us all some fresh coffee and we sat in the kitchen. I had the sense that the two officers didn't know how to begin. Obviously something was wrong, but I didn't know what. I thought it might be something insignificant, to do with our being twins, to do with one of us being mistaken for the other. It was a common occurrence for us. Maybe Kate had been shop-lifting again and someone had spotted her. She used to enjoy shop-lifting as a teenager. She always loved the challenge of getting away with it. Maybe she hadn't, this time.

She smiled conspiratorially at me. A 'here we go again' smile. We were more equal then. A day in the life of twins. Who had done what, this time?

'I'm afraid your parents are dead,' said the WPC.

What I remembered most clearly about this moment was Kate's face. The way it crumpled, like tissue-paper. The way it folded in on itself. As if it were a mask disintegrating. The mask of life. I felt I was watching mortality take place in a split second, as if standing outside time. I was watching Kate die.

But then she was resurrected. Beneath the mask was someone I had longed to find again. Someone I had known and loved. Someone to whom I belonged, and who belonged to me. Not just my own flesh and blood, but my own soul. Someone to keep and never to lose again.

Like everything else between us, she got there first. She understood before I did what the WPC had said.

'How?' she said.

'How?' I echoed, hearing the sentence consciously at last: *I'm afraid your parents are dead.*

Playing it back like a telephone message, and hearing it clearly now, I, too, understood what the policewoman said. I didn't believe it, but I understood what she was trying to say. I explained to her that it wasn't possible.

'Our parents are on holiday,' I said.

'I'm sorry, but they've been killed.'

I tried to explain to her as patiently as I could that our parents couldn't possibly have been killed since they were in South America. On holiday.

'What do you mean, they've been killed?' asked Kate, cutting through me.

'I'm sorry to say – they were in the wrong place at the wrong time,' the other police officer said. He thought he was better than his colleague at breaking difficult news, and he took over now. 'There was a shoot-out today at the airport in Buenos Aires.'

'Well, that's where they are,' I said, beginning to feel just a little uneasy now.

'That's right, miss, that's where they were.'

'Are,' I corrected. 'That's where they are.'

'Mo, will you just *shut up*!' Kate shouted at me.

The tears were rolling down her face like oceans of grief.

When I saw them I realized. I looked at the police officers.

'What happened?' I asked in a sudden half-voice, the other half out of control like the music on a cassette just before it is chewed up.

'They were in the way,' he said, 'caught in the cross-fire, I'm sorry to say. Between some drug-dealers and the police.'

I thought of them 'in the way'. I thought of their faces. I thought of them dropping their suitcases and wrapping themselves in each other's arms. And then I thought: they wouldn't even have known that they were going to die.

Kate was howling now.

'Who was the first to go?' I asked. I wanted the facts.

'They shot your mother first.'

I thought of her slipping out of Dada's arms. I thought of him trying to hold her up, trying to hold her alive, trying not to let her go. Trying not to be without her for as long as possible. I thought of the continuing cross-fire. I thought of Mama's body, bleeding on the ground.

'How quickly afterwards did they get my father?' I asked.

'They ... well, he – when he knew your mother was dead, he – well, he ran towards them, into the gunfire.'

'What are you saying?' blurted Kate through her tears.

'He ran towards them,' repeated the officer. 'He screamed at them.'

'So? Wouldn't you?' she asked.

'So they shot him.' He looked squarely at Kate. 'I'm sorry,' he said.

I thought of Dada running towards them. I thought of him shouting at them. I thought of the look in his eyes. I thought of him turning back to see the blood on Mama's clothes and shouting at them again, asking them to look at her, to see what they had done. I thought of the bullet in his chest, of his legs buckling under him. I thought of him struggling to walk. I thought of him collapsing on the ground. Did get back to Mama? Did he reach her in time? I tried to imagine that he did, but I couldn't quite see it. I couldn't quite think of any more.

'I can't tell you how sorry we are,' said the WPC. 'I wish we had some other kind of news to tell you.'

'Amen!' shouted Kate. 'Get out of my house now, will you?'

Her face was red with tears and it was clear that she blamed them.

'The trouble with your laws,' she said, 'is they do more harm than good.'

Epilogue

It is visitors' day today. I've come back to wait in my cell. Bill was due to arrive at two, but he's late. As usual. He never used to be late for appointments. But then, I never used to be a prisoner. Free people don't notice lateness so much. They can walk away and do something else.

Kate is dead now. After a long coma.

Howard is a prisoner too. Kate planted the evidence in his house on her last visit there (the same day that I saw her from my car). A knife. She got his fingerprints on the knife that killed Katherine. Howard says that she must have left it lying on his desk when he went to answer the door. I wish I hadn't knocked. Afterwards, she told the police about a knife that she had seen in his house. He only found it after she had gone. He didn't recognize it, so he picked it up to look at it, and put it down again.

He got a life-sentence for that.

In his last letter, over a month ago now, he said that he felt relieved in some ways to be a prisoner. 'Kate wanted the same power over me that Katherine had,' he said, 'but I could never give it to her. I've only ever made love to one other woman in my life,' he said, 'and that was you. As for the Plague,' he said, 'it is inside me. I have infected every woman who has ever loved me. I've turned each one into a killer. If a woman loves me, she is doomed. And, God help her, if I want her to love me, she will.'

Being famous, Neville Hoare's trial got a lot of publicity. So did mine, because mine was linked with his, and because Kate was famous too, but, relatively speaking, my trial hid in the shadow of his like a timid child in its mother's skirts. He gets a lot of post because of his fame, so he doesn't write as often as I would like. I miss him.

His father visits sometimes. He is trying to prove our innocence, which is nice of him, but he's not getting very far. I try not to pin too much hope on him, because he is old now and likely to die before any real progress is made. But I like to be believed.

Bill thinks I'm guilty. When he visits, we sit in silence for almost all of the time. And the time is so short. There is a look of such bewilderment in his eyes that I don't know where to begin.

READ MORE IN PENGUIN

In every corner of the world, on every subject under the sun, Penguin represents quality and variety – the very best in publishing today.

For complete information about books available from Penguin – including Puffins, Penguin Classics and Arkana – and how to order them, write to us at the appropriate address below. Please note that for copyright reasons the selection of books varies from country to country.

In the United Kingdom: Please write to *Dept. EP, Penguin Books Ltd, Bath Road, Harmondsworth, West Drayton, Middlesex UB7 ODA*

In the United States: Please write to *Consumer Sales, Penguin Putnam Inc., P.O. Box 999, Dept. 17109, Bergenfield, New Jersey 07621-0120.* VISA and MasterCard holders call 1-800-253-6476 to order Penguin titles

In Canada: Please write to *Penguin Books Canada Ltd, 10 Alcorn Avenue, Suite 300, Toronto, Ontario M4V 3B2*

In Australia: Please write to *Penguin Books Australia Ltd, P.O. Box 257, Ringwood, Victoria 3134*

In New Zealand: Please write to *Penguin Books (NZ) Ltd, Private Bag 102902, North Shore Mail Centre, Auckland 10*

In India: Please write to *Penguin Books India Pvt Ltd, 210 Chiranjiv Tower, 43 Nehru Place, New Delhi 110 019*

In the Netherlands: Please write to *Penguin Books Netherlands bv, Postbus 3507, NL-1001 AH Amsterdam*

In Germany: Please write to *Penguin Books Deutschland GmbH, Metzlerstrasse 26, 60594 Frankfurt am Main*

In Spain: Please write to *Penguin Books S. A., Bravo Murillo 19, 1° B, 28015 Madrid*

In Italy: Please write to *Penguin Italia s.r.l., Via Benedetto Croce 2, 20094 Corsico, Milano*

In France: Please write to *Penguin France, Le Carré Wilson, 62 rue Benjamin Baillaud, 31500 Toulouse*

In Japan: Please write to *Penguin Books Japan Ltd, Kaneko Building, 2-3-25 Koraku, Bunkyo-Ku, Tokyo 112*

In South Africa: Please write to *Penguin Books South Africa (Pty) Ltd, Private Bag X14, Parkview, 2122 Johannesburg*

READ MORE IN PENGUIN

A CHOICE OF FICTION

No Night is Too Long Barbara Vine

Tim Cornish, a creative-writing student, sits composing a confession: an admission of a crime committed two years ago that has yet to be discovered. 'A dark, watery masterpiece ... suffused with sexuality, which explores with hypnotic effect the psychological path between passion and murder' – *The Times*

Peerless Flats Esther Freud

Lisa has high hopes for her first year in London. She is sixteen and ambitious to become more like her sister Ruby. For Ruby has cropped hair, a past and a rockabilly boyfriend whose father is in prison. 'Freud sounds out as a clear, attractive voice in the literary hubbub' – *Observer*

One of the Family Monica Dickens

At 72 Chepstow Villas lives the Morley family: Leonard, the Assistant Manager of Whiteley's, his gentle wife Gwen, 'new woman' daughter Madge and son Dicky. Into their comfortable Edwardian world comes a sinister threat of murder and a charismatic stranger who will change their lives for ever. 'It is the contrasts that Dickens depicts so rivetingly ... she captures vividly the gradual blurring of social divisions during the last days of the Empire' – *Daily Mail*

Original Sin P. D. James

The literary world is shaken when a murder takes place at the Peverell Press, an old-established publishing house located in a dramatic mock-Venetian palace on the Thames. 'Superbly plotted ... James is interested in the soul, not just in the mind, of a killer' – *Daily Telegraph*

In Cold Domain Anne Fine

'A streamlined, ruthlessly stripped-down psychological family romance with enough plot twists and character revelations to fuel a book three times as long, as wicked and funny as anything Fay Weldon has written. Anne Fine is brilliant' – *Time Out*